£2
A25

The Bodyguard

ADRIAN MITCHELL

Allison & Busby
Published by W. H. Allen & Co. Plc

An Allison & Busby book
Published in 1988 by
W. H. Allen & Co. Plc
44 Hill Street
London W1X 8LB

Copyright © Adrian Mitchell 1970

Printed and bound in Great Britain by
Cox & Wyman Ltd, Reading, Berkshire

ISBN 0 85031 822 X

This book is sold subject to the condition that it shall
not, by way of trade or otherwise, be lent, re-sold, hired
out or otherwise circulated without the publisher's prior
consent in any form of binding or cover other than that in
which it is published and without a similar condition including
this condition being imposed upon the subsequent purchaser

I'M the product of social conditioning. Well, so are you and Jesus, who was odder than both of us put together. I can't see what kind of a man I am from inside all this conditioning, but perhaps you'll be able to judge, depending, I suppose, on your own social conditioning. My character's not beside the point, but the main point is my work as a bodyguard, because I'm one of the best in the world. I've never read a book by a bodyguard and I thought it was about time. I could've written a straight textbook, since my main intention is to assist young bodyguards, but I've always found that (a) I tend to forget the instructions given by textbooks and (b) I usually remember the stories in biographies. Also I would like to pass on to a wider public my experiences in the struggle against The Rot which threatens Britain and the civilized world. So I'll lie here – I'm in bed recovering from bullet wounds – and talk my way through my life into this tape-recorder and edit the tape when I've got time, sometimes talking rapidly and carelessly as the thoughts jump into my mind and out of my mouth, sometimes moving slowly, warily, trying to give each word its exact weight. My social conditioning includes the study of English Literature, so occasionally the language may even be striking. Inside every man there is a book struggling to get out, they say, and this is mine. I don't want to bore you, so I will skip the more commonplace aspects of my life and do my best to choose the more exotic episodes.

Social conditioning. I often think about it. I can't take my conditioning for granted, like breathing. What I am has been decided by a lot of different people, chances good and bad, institutions, friends and enemies. Also by my size, which I was born with. My own say in my character is harder to determine, but I think it has been small. Take my decision not to marry. This was a joint decision taken by my father, my schooling, my lower-than-average sexual drive and my vocation. I suppose I had a vote in this matter, but these outside forces made it one hundred times easier to avoid marriage.

My father was my first conditioner. My father, huge and white, clasping his tea-mug in his fist, striding over to the fireplace and kicking the coal into life – I am afraid of very few things, but even with my father dead for thirteen years, I'm nervous of writing about him, there's an ache which grows in my brain when I think about him. A very strong man he was, slicing slabs of clay from our garden with his spade, turning them over and beating them to pieces: sustained violence in shirtsleeves, the back of his great shaven neck glowing red in the afternoon – that's my father seen from an upstairs window. I was supposed to be working at my equations, but it was hot, my body wouldn't allow me to sit still, so I stared by the hour until he finally felt my eyes on his labour and he turned. I couldn't move from the window, he held my eyes, he stuck his spade into the ground and then he came indoors, slowly changed his boots for carpet-slippers, picked up his stick from the hallway, walked upstairs and then taught me to watch him.

My father was the Law. He was a policeman, publicly and privately. In his own home he maintained law and order in every detail: washing-up routines, bathroom discipline, treatment of beds, quietness on the stairs, behaviour, especially behaviour. The house stayed as he wanted it. Even the carpets seemed intimidated. He made the roses grow on time. At work my father was efficient and unsuccessful. He stayed in the ranks of the police and he knew why.

'They're afraid of me.'

Yes, and they were right, he had the eyes of hatred. He loved power – the books he read, the TV programmes he watched, his monologues – all of them were concerned with powerful men. So his superiors kept him down. His ferocity was useful to them but only while they pulled his strings. He must be allowed no authority or he would force his inferiors to become his disciples, his love and hate would swell, his hating eyes would spawn and multiply, he would break arms and wreck minds to force himself further towards the white-hot centre of power, the one sun he loved. If he had reached it there would have been a cosmic smell of burning and there is already too much burning in Britain. Somehow they explained this to him, even admitted their fear of him, judging rightly that his frustration would be matched by a new pride. There were enough leaders without my father, safer leaders, less inflammable, less aflame. I was in the room one day when a young officer told my father to keep his cool. My father had no cool to keep.

If I had been puny, I might well have rebelled against him. But I was born huge, fighting as I was born, killing my mother as I fought. And as I grew, in fear of my father, I gradually realized that one day I would be bigger and taller and stronger than him, that I might even outgrow my fear of him, who was everything I feared in the world. Some day perhaps. It wasn't a question of wanting to be like him – physically I was going to be him and more than him. It was only his failure which I rejected. Somehow my life had to work. I think that, with certain failures taken into account, it has worked.

For, leaping twenty years, some of which I'll colour in later, here I am at thirty-two, the best-known bodyguard in the

British Isles. I'm unknown to the public, but statesmen and security officers as well as subverts know the name of Len Rossman. Back in the early 'seventies, that might have been a limp kind of boast, but now in the mid-'eighties, there are maybe ten thousand fully trained and employed bodyguards (BGs) on Stateroll alone, quite apart from private BGs. The way the jungle mood of Europe's going, we'll end up with five times that number. Well, that's my personal prediction.

As I spoke that last sentence into my small microphone, I was suddenly aware of you reading it, perhaps many years later, and even at this early stage I'm worrying about what you think of me. It matters. I'm well aware that this book will be read by some people who will hate everything I stand for, for my opinions are strong. That's all right. Some of them will be people with whom I've tussled in the past or relatives of such people. But if they consider all the factors, they won't hate me. They really hate the men I've guarded, the men whom we BGs usually refer to as 'targets'. Each target is hated. I stand between the haters and the target they would like to hit. I anticipate their bullets or I deflect them bodily, but I also feel their hatred.

I don't dismiss hatred lightly. It is a very serious weapon. I believe that a politician, say the President of the USA, can be assassinated by hatred. Suppose nobody manages to get him with a gun, although his country is full of guns. His security weathermen warn him that the temperature is going to rise before the heat drops. So the President begins to confine his public appearances to military bases and so on, avoiding cities and open spaces, surrounded by BGs, the BGs surrounded by plain-clothes, the plain-clothes surrounded by cops and somewhere, way over in the distance, listening to the amplified voice of the President (but he is so far away it might not be the President at all) the ranks of uniformed men listening in tense silence to his words. Yes, physically, from the security point of view, the set-up might be a happy dream. Mentally or psychically, such a situation is a razor-slashed nightmare with eight legs. For year after year that man is constantly assaulted by cartoonists, foreign politicians from all but a droopy handful of 'allied countries', playwrights who see him as Dracula, newspapermen who have their liberal doubts about whether he is the ultimate gangster or simply ungentlemanly, and, perhaps most of all, he is assaulted by the inescapable fact that most of the people in the world hate him. That kind of massed, concentrated hatred is bad for a man. It rusts him. It rots him. I'm not over-sensitive, but if I'm up against a man who shows that he dislikes me strongly, that small rejection means a small loss of blood, of energy, of confidence, like when you chip your chin shaving. (My stubble is almost metallic.)

Now those who hate what I stand for will probably assume that, because of my job, I'm stupid. When De Gaulle was President of France, his bodyguards were called gorillas and that's the public image of the BG. And sometimes I have been stupid and sometimes I may sound stupid, my sentences may sometimes have to jerk round right-angled corners to arrive at their meaning. A good writer can gently swerve into a roundabout and out again, and you never notice. But don't let the style fool you. I'm ignorant, about a great many things I'm ignorant, but I'm not stupid enough to think I'm not ignorant. When I don't know about something, I'll tell you straight out – I'm not a newspaper.

I am not sophisticated, because although several of my targets and their friends have been sophisticated people, our mixing has been, with a few vivid exceptions, businesslike. Sophistication seems to be a matter of fashion and fashion is not central to my job. Perception is central. I'm cynical about extra-sensory perception, but I use it anyway. You know, that sudden scratch of danger when you feel sure it's an explosive suitcase, or the red-wigged duchess is really a man, or there's the cross of a rifle sight on the back of your neck. Whenever I feel that prickle, I act on it. And ninety-nine cases out of a hundred that ESP warning is lying or misinformed. Now some BGs put several tons of faith in ESP, but I think they forget about all the times when it flops. They certainly only tell you about that hundredth time.

Ordinary perception is different and more important. You can learn it. It's a matter of walking the length of a blazing, bright, pebbled beach and picking out the one stone which is not a stone. It's a matter of intensifying the focus of your eyes and brain at the same time, concentrating that focus and sweeping that beam of intensity backwards and forwards over a thousand people like a searchlight. And suddenly you stop the searchlight's swing. There is something about that man over there. He is, perhaps, too nervous. Or he's too calm. His eyes show traces of a drug. One of his hands makes it clear that he should not be at a diplomatic reception. One side of his jacket hangs lower than the other. You make sure to stand between him and the target you're protecting and then, if that nervous, calm, drugged, odd-handed or lopsided man moves just an inch to one side you watch him, without caring if he knows you're watching him, and without taking your eyes off him you beckon a plain-clothesman and send him to immobilize the potential assassin, all without speaking. Your plain-clothes won't necessarily arrest him, especially if it's one of those near-riot situations, he will stand over him, almost on top of him, jostling any lump in his clothing, of course, and generally making any threatening movement impossible.

Describe yourself in more detail.

Sure. When people compare me to anything, it's usually a bull or a brick wall. I prefer the former. To most men I must appear to be reasonably invulnerable to bare fists. Well, I do feel pain like anyone else, but I can take a lot more of it than your average. And dish out considerably more. I don't like pain any more than you do, but I'm probably less afraid of it. I have taken a couple of beatings. At the moment, of course, the bullet wounds hurt occasionally, but then the nurse gives me an injection. I can take these wounds, even the wound in my left eye. I forgot to tell you, my eyes are bandaged over because of that wound. Anyway, I'd rather have these wounds than cancer any day. Again, the idea of death doesn't frighten me in the least. I don't get sentimental about the prospect of my own death and I don't get worked up about other people's deaths. Well, very rarely. If I read of (say) policemen being killed in a riot and I never knew those particular cops, I don't get angry like most other ex-cops. What's the point of anger like that? I remember the facts of course, I store them up, I might hit a little harder or shoot a little quicker next time something breaks, but it would be in cold vengeance, not in anger. I fight better cold, I can aim straighter. And I believe in revenge as a useful tactic. Anger is a nuisance which disturbs the faculties. It upsets your balance. I have seen angry cops and Yellows in action and they're not efficient. They hit at the wrong time, the Rot mob swallows them and then sicks them out again with bad noses and ears, or dead.

My own time as an ordinary cop was solid and never particularly spectacular. I kept quiet and moved from department to department whenever I could, trying to pick up the tricks. My father had retired to solitary anger by the time I joined and the force he loved and loathed was changing fast. Traffic duties had been placed in the hands of the Warden Force. The Civil Police had been set up, part-time and plain-clothes, glorified street- and parish-informers really, but with two weeks' a year training and a pension scheme – the ideal Civil Cop is a pub landlord or the porter of a block of flats. Nice thing about them is that you never know if your best friend is one of them or not. There may be a hundred thousand of them, there are certainly at least twenty-five thousand. They take a load off the police proper, but of course I was never in that mob. Eventually I graduated to the European Riot Police. While I was with them—

You'd better describe them.
Everyone knows about the Yellows.
Just for the record.

Sure, well the Yellows got to be something of a legend, yes a powerful legend. They were set up by the European Community Parliament to deal with The Rot. European Riot Police – the ERPs – but everyone calls them the Yellows. Let's stop and inspect a Yellow. He stands in the changing-room of his base, naked from the shower. Larger than most men, with the long thin smile of his kind, hair cropped down to stubble. First he straps on his under-armour, partly derived from the American footballer – wide shoulder-pads, almost invulnerable groin-protector, shin-pads. Next his ordinary pants and his semi-bullet-proof, heavy-duty shirt with its breathing holes. The shirt is mustard yellow, so are the socks which follow, so are the simulated leather trousers and the similar battle jacket, joined in the front with studs, easy to remove if it catches fire. Now the goggles, two slanted ovals padded with yellow leather, occasionally worn on the forehead, but usually, in and out of action, across the eyes, the flat lenses slightly tinged with yellow. Everything looks yellow to a Yellow. Next the helmet, an extremely tough, but comparatively light, yellow shell, padded inside and protecting an arc from the upper forehead to the back of the neck. Now our man checks his routine equipment – pocket radio, watch, concealed knives (two) and, slightly more conventionally for a cop, notebook and pen. They're all right. He sits down and pulls on his boots, yellow boots, hard as steel on the outside but fitting beautifully, good for running and better for kicking, tested by leading soccer players. He puts on his belt, with its handcuffs, gas grenades and aerosol. Around the back his emergency mini-napalm eggs. Ammo belt clipped over one shoulder. Around his neck, ready to be donned in two seconds flat, his respirator with its little box of oxygen. Then, with slightly awkward movements of his shoulders, he pulls on his trademark, the thick, voluminous yellow mac, belted at the waist where his revolver and shriek-whistle hang. Now he is insulated against too much heat, too much cold or too much violence. He takes down his long night-stick in its black holster and clips it to his belt. And now he's nearly complete, ready to report to the armoury for his automatic rifle, grenade rifle, sub-machine-gun or whatever the authorities have decided shall be his weapon today. He gives an impression of alien bulk and weight, a robot with murder in its yellow blood. He collects his weapon, he tests it, he pulls on his gauntlets. He goes out to join the other yellow giants.

The Yellows call themselves the Yellows, proudly. The public also call them the Yellows, but with some fear. They come from every nation in the Community – when I did a stint in Belgium I had a Portuguese Commandant and a German Deputy. The main advantage of such a mixture is obvious – it's not so worrying to fire on a foreign crowd. The language problem is unimportant – all orders are standardized in English and you have to know the phrase-book back to front, foreign or not. The Yellows made their first British appearance in Glasgow, a test run. They cleaned up a city-wide, general-strike meeting in fifteen minutes. There had been no warning. That night the hospitals were packed, but all other public places were deserted as the Yellows patrolled the streets in their prowlers. There was no need to declare a curfew, the Glaswegians took one look at the Yellows, saw that they were hopelessly out-armoured and outgunned, and, except for a few unfortunate drunks, stayed indoors. A great success. The All-Party Government realized that if the Yellows could subdue Glasgow, they could subdue anything short of Armageddon.

Glasgow was followed by other operations, some small, some large, in Bristol, Blackburn, Hull, Cardiff, Wolverhampton and London. The TV newsreels were fantastic. Within a year there were two best-selling paperbacks about the Yellows, five TV documentaries, one feature film and at least two newsreel appearances a week. The legend sank in quickly. In the more broken towns of the Midlands and the North especially, big posters appeared everywhere – the huge figure of a Yellow charging (a hundred other Yellows suggested just behind him by the artist) and the words: JOIN THE ERP. But it wasn't really a recruiting poster, it was a warning, a reminder of that rhinoceros man aiming himself at your head or your groin. The posters in sophisticated towns were more abstract, showing a yellow wedge of diamond shapes bursting into a fleeing crowd of ragged, different-coloured shapes. The words said: SAVING OUR SOCIETY – THE EUROPEAN RIOT POLICE.

At first the middle-middle class and those above them were keen on the Yellows. The honeymoon was brief. Of course the solid citizen doesn't attend strike meetings or demos, but the solid citizen is used to moving about pretty damn freely in his car. He doesn't appreciate Yellow roadblocks. A Yellow never calls you sir. A Yellow gives orders. Yellows smile through you, not at you. And if you happen to have mislaid your ID card, or try to be funny or patronizing or stroppy or important, a Yellow won't worry about your class rating with the advertising fraternity before he cuts you down to size in a straightforward, painful manner. If you happen to be walking out of your club while the Yellows are mopping up the street, you are likely to be mopped. So the national habit started – if you see a patch of yellow at the end of the street you turn back, or veer down a side street, or suddenly decide to go to the cinema or the bank or the launderette, whichever happens to be nearest. And if the Yellows come into your pub, you drink up quietly and leave politely. If you stay you find yourself, if you're lucky, buying a series of large and expensive rounds. Motorists tend to avoid the roads on which Yellow camps are sited, which is possible, because most of them are outside towns, usually down side roads. I even encountered one man, a grocer, who took refuge in a police station to avoid being taken to a Yellow camp for questioning. An imaginative move, but of course it didn't work.

They say that the colour yellow was chosen by a panel of neurologists, advertisers and witch-doctors who pondered its associations with pus, with vomit, with mustard gas (that takes you back a bit doesn't it) and even with peril. The magic worked. Yellow became, throughout Europe, Scandinavia to Sicily as they say, an unlucky colour. Yellow clothes went permanently out of fashion. A publisher found that nobody bought books with yellow covers because people found it unpleasant or unlucky to touch yellow paper. Every daffodil in the country became an advertisement for fear. It was a deliberately disseminated and useful neurosis. I doubt if we'd have pulled through the 'seventies without the Yellows.

To tell you the truth, I wasn't satisfied with my future in the Yellows. I wanted to be an important part of the country's security system, but I wanted to use my brain as well as my body and I wanted to be an individual, not a yellow diamond among yellow diamonds. One day I was part of a Yellow guard at a conference of bankers. There must have been thirty of us around the hall, but I was with five others, occupying the long oblong room outside the conference chamber. There was no trouble in the streets and no sign of trouble. In fact we were chatting, swigging tea and eating small cakes with cherries on top. Mostly the talk was soccer. But I wasn't listening to the others, I was watching. A man of six foot five, repeat, six foot five, with big eyes and a finely cut suit was leaning against the wall. He was in the same room as us, but obviously he was from another world. His lengthy arms were folded and he was doing nothing. He noticed immediately that I was watching him. After ignoring me for five minutes, he looked at his watch and nodded. I walked over. He spoke rapidly and quietly.

'They'll be out in ten minutes. Better search the caterers.'

'That's all right,' I said, 'we searched them earlier.'

'Search them again. They could've got weapons since then. Anyway, I didn't see you search them. Watch the one with the nose.'

It made sense. I took two other Yellows and we went through the caterers, finding a revolver on the one with the nose. We arrested the lot and sent them out to be thrown in the prowlers. The tall man nodded at me again.

'Learn anything?'

'Yes. We should have been watching.'

'Not your speciality. I'm a BG. My field.'

'You mean we're just the muscle.'

'Are you?'

'That's all we're expected to be.'

I was impressed by the man and he was impressed by me.

'I don't think you're a thug,' he said. 'You should do some time at Hollow Hill.'

At that time I'd never heard of Hollow Hill, but I didn't let on because (*a*) I didn't want to seem stupid and (*b*) it was obviously the sort of place about which you shouldn't ask strangers. But I spent some time during the next few weeks finding out. The first word was that it was a BG training school in Wiltshire, which encouraged me, as I think of Wiltshire as a county where dedicated men learn serious trades like war among bleak, treeless hills. Wiltshire also has Stonehenge which has always appealed to me, and I respect the army traditions of Salisbury Plain although I was never in the army proper. Second thing I found was that I qualified for entry to the Hill on my past exam results, but that the course was complicated and tough. More experience would give me a better chance. If I failed once, I felt, I would never pass. The more I heard about the place, the more confusing Hollow Hill sounded. No two men gave the same description of their courses and the only common factor, whether the narrator had liked the place or not, was an air of danger which crept into their voices when they talked about it. The style of their conversation, at any rate, made me feel that I wasn't yet good enough.

But the mention of the word 'thug' by that tall man, whose name was Finn Murdoch, scraped me. It was true, the Yellows are, have to be, will always be, in some sense, thugs. The image of the six of us, chewing cakes, thinking soccer, wearing that bulky, septic yellow under the fine gaze of Finn, consciously and elegantly alert, kept returning to my mind. Six yellow clowns we must have seemed to him, six yellow thugs. So I started going to night-school, the first step on my journey to Hollow Hill. I worked well, I've never needed much sleep. My teacher, who I suspect was an old subvert at heart, took me for a drink after my eighth week and confessed finally that although he'd been afraid of me at first because of my physical bulk, my essays had finally convinced him that there was a brain lurking under my skull. I kept my temper, but sometimes I feel as if I go through life sporting a T-shirt marked PHYSICAL BULK. To me that's an ugly phrase, and I twist my mouth whenever I see or hear it. Better than puny, better than skinny, of course, but there's a great deal of anti-bulk prejudice around. To hard men I represent a challenge, and in several of the tougher pubs I've been called on to perform against the local champion, which interrupts my peaceful evening. To most people I represent a threat simply by looming, nothing more. If I hold my head up when I walk into a room, I'm mentally marked down as a brute and bruiser by half the onlookers. If I hang my head they think I'm a moron. I won't hang my head. My bones are big, but my brain's not small. For my purposes, however, it's not always a bad thing if I'm thought of as stupid or slow-witted, it can give me a secret weapon. I can move fast, especially over short distances, because I'm not afraid to crash into a wall or a man, I'm not afraid to hurtle.

With women, the physical bulk effect is odd. It seems to attract either very small or very frightened or very stupid women, but whatever the adjectives, they are all women. That's good enough for me, that'll do. I don't understand women and I never need them overwhelmingly. They seldom interest me, except for occasional sex, and I can, what with the stupid, the frightened and the small, get all I need of that whenever I want. But I can never take very seriously the fact that way down below, my loins are discharging a tea-spoonful of weight. I know perfectly well that this is unusual, and perhaps it's even horrible to many people (especially women) but I've always felt a kind of detachment from my genitalia, as if their needs were quite different from my own needs. I'm quite fond of them, all the same.

Anyway, Physical Bulk didn't keep me out of Oxford. The top Yellows decided I should go as an *agent provocateur* and, using my night-school diploma, they fixed me an industrial scholarship and a place at Balliol. During my first few days thirty students must have rapped on my door and invited me to join their clubs. I was ready for them. My shelves sported subvert books and a revolutionary rag with several paragraphs underlined lay on my coffee-table. I think it was the Chess Club lad who passed the word back, or it could have been the New Labour Party boy, to whom I made a short and violent speech attacking the recently announced All-Party Government to be formed by the New Labour Party, the New Conservatives and the New Liberals. I even used the correct subvert term for the coalition – the Slagheap. Other visitors began to call. The Anglican-Methodist rep looked to me like a fellow agent, but of course I didn't try to find out, I kept up my red front. There's probably a government department somewhere with a political profile of me that makes Trotsky look like Little Bo-Peep. That's a joke, really. Anyway, I didn't even want to know if the Anglo-Meth was an agent or not. Best to carry on as if you're the only agent in the world.

The first subvert circle I reached was a milkily legal discussion group made up of talkers who were going to stay that way. Mostly they discussed the Russian Revolution, and most of their theory and history stopped at about 1950. They seemed too scared to face the present or the future. They spoke like dust. If they'd had the guts to have a group photograph taken, it would have come out like an abstract painting. There was nothing much for me to do with this group except (*a*) record their names and pass them on for future round-ups in subvert emergencies and (*b*) establish myself a reputation as a mystery man of action, red as hell and let's stuff all this chat.

I was interrogated genteely for hours over tea-cups – without anyone acknowledging that I was being dredged. I was taken to a Walton Street party, pretended to get drunk and was taken to a backroom and incited to flights of violent political fantasy by a kid called David who kept telling me to whisper. Then, pretending to go for a piss, he came back with a girl called Josie whom I'd never seen before, so, still acting the drunk, I changed the subject and refused to be drawn into any politics at all, thus impressing them as a reliable man.

Eventually I reached the second circle. This was a cell of subverts. Mixed denominations, but all six of them, including David and Josie, were cool and intellectual, mimeographing and distributing an illegal paper which they didn't even write. (Usual sentence: three years' rehabilitation.) These kids were dedicated, very disciplined and not given to gossip or too many abstractions. Their paper didn't have much sting, being packed with exposures of oppression abroad, but pretty reticent when it came to the actions of The Rot in Britain. None of the six was officially in charge, they consciously avoided exercising even the authority of their own personalities over each other, but Josie, despite herself, was the one with the political magnetism. She sat in her room one afternoon, small and brunette. She had her hair tied back and she was typing at a table. No pictures on the walls, a few chemistry books on her shelves, some wild flowers here and there in jam-jars. I made some instant coffee for us while she finished her essay on enzymes. Then I sprung it on her.

'Bad news.'

'Usually is.'

'The Yellows shot up the strikers at Barrow.'

'You know any more?'

'They were aiming. They killed Linnell.'

'Jesus blood.'

'Two others dead. Fifteen wounded.'

'They can't – well, of course, they can. You sure?'

'Right. Friend was there. I saw him. He's all right.'

'When did you see him? I'm sorry. Shouldn't ask.'

'I'd better write up the story for the rag then?'

'You could.'

'Of course I've got to.'

'Look, you can't be sure they'll print it, that's all.'

'It's not going to be printed anywhere else. Not till the Media Police turn Red.'

'One of the rags would do it. There's a bloke in the Midlands. I'll get it to him if you like.'

'But we've got a real circulation.'

'That's right. We've also got limits. I don't like it, love, but for the time being I work with it. Limits. Look, I'll explain, I may be sick in the middle of it—'

'Me too.'

'Until things get rougher, which they will, we're probably not going to be busted. *If* we avoid breaking the wrong kind of stories. People being shot in England is the wrong kind. Argentina – that's OK. New Zealand – blaze away. But nobody gets shot in Barrow, or anywhere else in the European Community for that matter, except by accident or in self-defence.'

'They're shooting them down somewhere in Europe every day of the week.'

'Only subverts believe that.'

'Everyone believes it in Barrow.'

'Oh yeah, but Barrow's a write-off for the State, always been subvert and rolling downhill every year. The Slagheap doesn't give a fuck what happens in Barrow, so long as Barrow dies in the end.'

'But if everyone in Barrow knows—'

'The media aren't going to blab and if they don't blab nobody believes it. Just a Red rumour. Most people don't even know where Barrow is and if they do know they think it's packed with subverts, which it is—'

'Lot of people knew Linnell.'

'A lot of subverts knew Linnell. But he wasn't famous. Not a personality. You never got his face on TV.'

'You know damn well we ought to print.'

'I don't decide. Anyway, this isn't a bloody 'thirties movie about New York newspapermen, you know damn well they can file us away in a camp any time they like. We do what we can, that's what we do, Len.'

Then Josie put her arms round me, for which I had to lean down. She shook for a time before she could manage to start crying. Her breasts were extremely hot, through her blouse and my shirt. It was perfectly obvious what she wanted. With Josie hanging round my chest, I walked over to the door and locked it, then backed up to the sofa, sat both of us down and began to think myself into the necessary state of mind. This involved clearing Josie right out of my brain, easy enough, and then introducing Technicolor nude images from a Channel 13 comedy series about a nudist colony together with a soundtrack stolen from an old Maupassant story I read about a Frenchman who questions a chambermaid about her mistress. She answers all his questions until he asks her about the lady's figure. She answers something like: 'Her figure is just like mine.' So that night the Frenchman hides behind the chambermaid's door and when she comes to bed he grabs her, investigates her body and discovers that unless the girl is lying, the lady's figure must be very good indeed. It's a dopy sort of story and there's more to it than that, but that's the bit I like and it seldom fails to excite me. For a setting I transferred the whole action to a wooden hotel in the middle of the Arizona desert. With the help of this scenario I was able to cope with Josie once, twice and, after a pause of a few hours, a third, conclusive time. In between she worried about Barrow and I murmured something about revenge.

For I'd come to the university to plant one word and then to watch it grow. I know as well as you do that years ago that word was pronounced to be dead. But colour TV in every room or not, words retain an odd strength. Even today the echoes of a coined slogan, Black Power, are still shaking around the world. Just two words colliding, exploding down the years. And the nicest thing about the word I had been carrying and now delivered into Josie's care was that it hadn't been used seriously in Britain for many years – revenge. A short word, short enough to be lipsticked on the brow of a dead Yellow. A muscular word. A vibrant word. I take no credit for it, the word was given to me by Security.

The first meeting of Revenge took place on a tatty island in the Isis, chosen because it couldn't possibly be bugged and of course the island itself wasn't bugged. The bug was sewn neatly into my jacket. There were six of us, but only Josie and I were from the second circle, the others were new to me. Josie spoke first, a maddened speech saying that reprisals should be taken every time the Yellows struck. Then she contradicted this by saying that we must stick to six members only. I let a flop-haired boy with heavy spectacles blow up that one, by pointing out that one team of six couldn't hope to get far with sabotage or cop-killing – each one of us should form his own team. I put in that if we did that, we must coordinate, much better to strike in six places on the same night than to concentrate on individual strikes. Josie was pleased by the way the discussion was turning, the faces around were reddening, and she agreed that after a raid in which all six of us should take part, we should each form our own team. She offered to produce any bombs we needed, chemistry being her game. I said that it would be bloody hard to form six teams of six, there weren't enough fanatics like us. A quiet Indian undergraduate called Sunil claimed to know four good men. Some names were dropped. I mentioned David, who was dismissed by two votes as a possible agent for Security. More names followed.

Next stage was deciding where to strike. Josie said that an eventual aim should be to break through into a Rehabilitation Camp, freeing its prisoners. But we should first aim at a more modest installation, provided it had an accessible armoury. We certainly weren't ready for an American or a European military base. Even the big police stations were built like fortresses. But a concerted raid on one of the small Yellow camps dotted around the countryside would certainly result in some good modern arms and a bit of revenge on the side. It had never been done.

At our second meeting we spent several hours on maps, selecting the right Yellow base, choosing the caches for captured weapons, thinking about transport, alibis and what to do in case of accidents. The names of two doctors were quoted. Then we all looked at each other. I could see they were afraid. We still had to fix the time and date. Josie said that it shouldn't be decided straight away, just one of them should decide it and let the others know at the last minute. At 11 PM every night from now on each member of Revenge should be at home and ready. The word would come.

The flop-haired boy said, 'Good security. Josie, why don't you and Len work it out between you?'

She looked at me and I made a why-not face. Revenge was going well. Next day we drove out together, acting the roles of rural lovers, at least I was acting, to hold a reccy on the Yellow camp. It was an L of concrete paths and huts, vulnerably sited below a wooded hill. When you looked down through binoculars, those yellow shapes became men. Men at 10 AM emerging from a lecture hut, pushing each other out of the way as they mobbed the coffee machines, followed by a civvy lecturer in a dated leather jacket. Men at 10.30 AM marching at the double with controlled violence and the full terrifying gear, pounding over the tarmac square at the bottom end of the L. Men at 11.30 AM shrugging as they crowded back for another lecture or maybe a film. Men at 12.30 PM jostling into the cookhouse, just to the left of the lecture theatre. Men at 1 PM belching beans on their way back to their billets. And in the joint of the L, six men, with yellow blancoed belts, marching without weapons into a small square hut, marching with weapons out of it and sixteen paces across to the guardhouse. The new guard. The armoury was only twenty paces from the entrance to the camp, two men on guard and four in the guardhouse. We only needed a few revolvers and several grenades. Only one road led out of the camp. The countryside beyond was a maze of minor roads. Around 2 PM we made some sort of love in the wood. Then Josie set the time and date of the attack. I said it sounded right to me. What's the matter?

Nothing. It's just that a lot of people who read your book won't know how The Rot was composed at that time. Hadn't you better say something about the other subvert groups?

Good idea. Then I'll come back to that raid, right?

Fine.

Of course Revenge was only one of a hundred sabotage/assassination groups being set up at the same time, many of them by agents. Our idea was to pull a net through the entire subvert movement and throw onto the deck a good percentage of the killer fish. I had no twinges, not having been trained to be a gentleman. And I knew plenty about the Subvert Movement, The Rot. Subverts came in all shapes and sizes, some were merely eccentric, but some were genuinely anti-State. I'll list some of the more active groups of that time.

Nearest to Revenge were, I suppose, the Tylers, picturesquely named after Wat Tyler but having little in common with him apart from their failure to win. They were a group dedicated to hit-and-run tactics, boasting they could materialize as an armed mob in five minutes and evaporate in one. They were dangerous in a microscopic way, existing mainly in the North of England, Scotland, Wales and the ghettoes.

Arson was a totally destructive group whose aim was to destroy property, public and private. Very small cells, only two or three strong. During the 'seventies they became very accomplished technically, and fires due to such groups accounted for the 120 per cent rise in damage to public property by fire in 1978. The number of arrests was low. This was partly because

Arson was composed of fanatical specialists who made it a matter of principle to engage in no other subvert activities. You never found them in discussion groups. There were factions within Arson. But basically they hated objects – something they shared with old-fashioned vandals. Even the explosion of a light bulb in a train appeared to give them some satisfaction, but only destruction by fire seemed to meet their need for an image of – what? – revolution, the pain they felt inside themselves or the grand old bomb. I'd like to have questioned some of those lads, they interested me.

The Urban Guerrillas were similar to the Tylers, but they tended to attack military bases. High fatality rate. There was no mucking about with this group. If they so much as tampered with the wire round a base, they were shot down. But they didn't only attack the bases. They also attacked and killed a number of European and US troops when they were off-duty, sometimes by using fake prostitutes, sometimes by bomb attacks in clubs, etc. This two-pronged attack meant a steep increase in military manpower – we've never needed more than a token defence force for bases in Britain before – and this diverted valuable troops and arms from the front lines of Latin America and Asia.

The Cold Regiment started when conscription was re-introduced to cope with the increasingly heavy burden of the Alliance. Most conscripts did not object – well they grumbled, but as usual they went. But the Cold Regiment had agreed among themselves to enter the forces quietly, obtain the highest ranks available and work from within to disrupt and disaffect the armed services. Like most other genuinely subvert bodies, they appear to have had no national coordinating body. Their aim, revealed by interrogated members of the Cold Regiment, was a coup which would grant power to a coalition of Rot groups. They would have been easier to destroy if they'd been better organized.

Shadow is harder to explain, it was less a political movement than a mythology. In subvert conversation and writing, you kept coming across references to The Shadow State, a grotesque parody of the Community. There was, apparently, a Shadow Royal Family given to monstrous though wraith-like orgies and the counting of money made of ashes, a Shadow Army which held surrealist parades on beaches and car-parks, a Shadow Police who carried transparent truncheons, a Shadow Air Force which held fly-pasts at dusk and Shadow Banks which were only open to gangsters. You'd be walking through a suburban allotment and the twentieth ramshackle hut you passed would be painted with the words: KEEP OUT. THIS IS A SHADOW PRISON. An old boiler, weighing several tons and painted silver, was found one morning in the town square of Bury St Edmunds. Along its side the words said: DO NOT MOVE. MOVE NOTHING. MOVEMENT IS FORBIDDEN. THIS IS THE SHADOW DOOMSDAY MACHINE. It was just an old boiler, of course. They even had an irregular newspaper, in which I read a review of a performance of *The Shadow Magic Flute* at the Shadow Royal Opera House, Covent Garden.

I once took part in a Yellow raid on a restaurant where men and women, rather smartly dressed, sat around and, by candle-light, ate their own shit, but I could never see political significance in that. You really had to class those nuts with the almost entirely a-political drugland folk. Take the Katheads for instance. They took Kat, a solid drug which sends the user into a trance characterized by sitting still, staring and shaking. Eventually, at some sort of psychic crisis, the Kathead would howl for some time, then keel over and sleep. These howls were often recorded, since they were highly valued by other Katheads as well as Katfanciers, who were not users, but just liked to watch and listen.

The Boulders believed that the ideal state of man was to sit in one place and react to nothing outside. When forced to move, they would put their arms round their knees, tuck in their heads and roll – a sort of joke, and their only joke. Boulders took turns as Baiters, testing each other's resistance to tickling, fire, pins, etc. They tended to wear grey body make-up, in an attempt to look like stones. There was a rumour of one Boulder who pebble-dashed himself. Boulders inhaled a sense-stultifying gas called JJ–6. This was sold in plastic capsules known as jays (or sometimes buds from the plastic bud which had to be nipped off with the teeth or scissors).

The Mikes were really loony, and dangerous with it. They believed that the human body should be destroyed and that microbes should be encouraged to inherit the earth. Their idea was to work towards a point of decision – the Ledge they called it – at which a man could look at his body with such contempt that he would inject it with disease. The more diseases and the more dangerous they were, the greater the honour among Mikes. It was sometimes the practice to go over the Ledge and then clamber back with quick antidotes, anti-biotics, etc, but this was only admired if, as soon as recovery was certain, the Mike made straight for the Ledge again. There were also Missionary Mikes whose aim was to spread disease by injecting something contagious and then mixing in crowds. This was straight madness, but it was fashionable for a time.

What about John Custard?

Yes. Well he was one of those odd characters. You could never really be sure if there was a John Custard or not, there were plenty of stories about him, but he was something of an escapologist. He never stood trial so how can anyone be sure that he ever existed? Maybe John Custard was simply a number of people who used the same bloody ridiculous tactics. I'll come back to him.

Obviously an exhaustive survey of The Rot would have to include the banned, old-established parties like the New Maoists, the Old Maoists, Cubans, Trots, etc, etc, but the Registration of Parties Act had effectively and suddenly swept them under the carpet, where they lurked, breathing dust. Most of their members were active in one or several of the organizations I've already described. I should also mention, lightly, certain members of the New Labour Party known to be sympathetic with The Rot, but so thoroughly compromised by their positions in the All-Party or Community Parliaments that they were about as threatening to the State as convolvulus. They were watched. The churches were mostly positive.

Well, I've gone on for a long time and hardly covered one tenth of the movements which composed The Rot. I want to help contain and eventually eliminate The Rot. I have never dreamed of power or wealth for myself. But I have dreamed of an England and a Europe which are both strong and clean.

You were talking about the attack on the Yellow camp.

Yes. My watch with Josie lasted for twenty-four hours. It looked as if ten minutes to three in the morning should be the best time, there were other possible times for an attack, but that was the one we preferred. Yes. I know this is silly, but at this point I want to say that I sometimes feel as if I am dictating this against my will. I think it may be something to do with my injections.

The injections stop the pain from your wounds.

Yes. But they make me talk, too, they make me want to talk.

My memory, which is, was, always good, is clearer than usual. The past seems more vivid than the present. I am dictating this against my will.

I want to say it all. I don't want to say anything.

Let me get back to that attack on the Yellow camp, I'm sorry that's the second diversion, I mean digression. There was one more meeting at the island, this time with an exact map of the camp. Of course, we plotted it out like a military operation as they say, because from the point of view of Revenge it was a military operation, as if Revenge knew anything about military operations. They're beginning to hurt again.

I'll ring for the nurse. Better have another injection.

Sorry. Ah, yes, that's better. The attack. As planned we drove to a hotel a few miles out of Oxford and stole a car from the car park, an estate wagon it was. I started it with a tug at a wire in the engine. I drove the wagon and Sunil drove his own car, which was souped up and good for a getaway, old mud on the numberplates, all that. The road began to wind about two miles before the base. As we rounded the second bend the road was barred by a heavy wooden pole on trestles. It was painted yellow. There had been no warning roadblock sign. The block was manned by an officer and six Yellows with shining super-stens. Our routine for a roadblock was clear. Our pistols and grenades were strapped under Sunil's car. Then six more Yellows appeared, just too soon. Josie swore, it was now clear that this was no ordinary roadblock. Sunil knew it and began to U-turn, but the Yellows began to laugh, the road was too narrow, he was half into the ditch and just throwing his gear into reverse when one of them took two paces forward and shattered his near-side rear wheel. Sunil and the three others in his car opened the doors and began to run for it. They must have known what would happen, but apparently it scared them less than a Yellow interrogation. The super-stens ripped them apart as they ran. Josie and I crouched low in the wagon. By now she was making grunting pig noises. A pair of slanted goggles stared in at us, the door was pulled open, a smiling mouth said: 'Walk.' Side by side we walked to the prowler.

Next day they flew me to Madrid for a holiday. There was no question of my going back to Balliol. Pity. As far as Oxford was concerned, I'd been swallowed alive by the Yellows. They even printed a protest pamphlet demanding my release, along with Josie's and the others'. I've got a copy somewhere. I did hope they'd take it easy on Josie. She had a nice body. Several years later a Yellow officer told me that they'd kept her at the camp for two months before sending her off for rehabilitation. Well, I know there are a lot of hard cases in the Yellows, but they're not all like that. Anyway, Josie was a bloody dangerous subvert; well, she would have been.

It was hot in Spain. I travelled in a coach with green windows to some port and in a hovercraft to Ibiza, where I was met by a Fiat and driven through the dust to a group of cool white chalets round a fine pink-painted building. It was a rest camp for State-roll employees. The campers were unlike normal holiday-makers in that they were fitter, neater and had no children. The place probably had less security precautions than your average holiday camp, at least it looked that way, any precautions were kept out of sight. Some of the men were presumably Yellows, some of the women certainly looked like agents, but you were never sure, the place, which was called Port Light, had only one strict rule – nobody talked shop.

That first evening in Port Light, I remember standing alone in my chalet, admiring its cleanliness. There was very little in the room, and I liked that. A large bed, a woven rug on the orange-tiled floor, clothes-hangers behind a green curtain, wash-basin, bedside table and a shower. Through the window I could see, about three miles away, a single sail, then, moving fast and close across my view, the half-turned tanned shoulder and head of a man who laughed with some companion, a girl I could not see. There were four clouds, bright white at their centres and vague at the edges. All the air was warm, and without thinking why I took off my shoes and socks and felt the lukewarm glassiness of the tiles under my soles. I let my jacket drop in a heap. Perhaps this is the best moment in my life, I thought at the time. Then another thought came into my head – that I'd been suffering from regular headaches for years and had hardly noticed them, accepting them as part of everyone's life, but now, with my first real holiday, my head was telling me something odd, that although it still ached, the ache was different, the ache had moved and that even this new ache was dissolving rapidly and would soon be gone. It was as if my skull had been frozen, or filled with spikes of ice for many years, and now it was beginning to melt. The ache moved down into my throat. I couldn't believe what it was. I wanted to take off all my clothes, but there wasn't time. I was half out of my shirt when I had to throw myself on the bed to silence the sobs which were radiating from that ache in my throat. Falsetto cries, like some animal. I hadn't cried since I was ten.

When I was able to stop crying, I discovered that I was happy. The ice age was over. I showered and sang gently to myself, my body feeling like the rocks in a waterfall. Then I put on my black suit and strolled over to the central hall. I like this place, I said to myself, and I'm going to like it even more. The inside of the hall suddenly opened into a darkened cave about the size of two swimming-pools side by side. Voluminous, wafting blue curtains. Small coloured lights at random points on the walls. Candle-lit tables around the edges of the area, a quiet band set on a marble platform – I wish, in some ways, I was there now. A waiter took me over to a table where seven men and women sat, some munching paella, some simply drinking and talking. We introduced ourselves and within five minutes I was talking about films with a green-eyed girl from Purley, but I wasn't thinking about my words, I was calculating nothing, just letting a few sentences roll and drift out of the side of my mouth when there was too much silence, drinking in the air of the place, the taste of the company, the wine and most of all an odd sense of wonder.

These faces around me were different from – I was going to say the faces on earth – but I mean the faces back in England. Perhaps I imagined it, but they seemed to have certainty in common. Some of them were tired faces, yes, what do you expect in a rest camp, but whether the skin of those faces was tired or tanned, the eyes were sure. It was the relief of having cried at last, it was the thought that I'd been chosen to share this little Valhalla, because that was the comic-book word which sprung into my mind as I sat easily and looked from table to table, imagining horned helmets on those steady heads, it was a renewed sense of mission and it was also the cold yellow wine – I was happy.

As the drummer gave a final roll and crash and the musicians began to disperse, a man I recognized swung through the doors of blue glass edged with glowing copper. Even in the jungle light I could tell who it was by the cut of his suit, by his height, by the sharp silhouette of his face. He was Finn Murdoch, the bodyguard I'd met at the bankers' conference, but tonight he was drunk or high, moving like a skater without skates on independently suspended legs. For a second I felt like a husband, wife or parent, anxious to know how society would judge him as he wandered from table to table, looking at each face, nodding now and then. I was relieved. Nobody minded, they greeted him. Twice it looked as if he would lurch over a table, but each time one of his legs reacted efficiently to his brain's message that balance was being lost, and each time he managed to accomplish a handshake without disaster or offence. And then he was leaning over my table, stretching over my shoulder to kiss the hand of the green-eyed girl. I worried about whether he would know me. He'd only seen me once before, my helmet covering my hair, goggles perched on my forehead and solid yellow from my boots to my chin. He looked at me, did a double-take, then pointed a long forefinger at my nose.

'You're, you're Thug from the bankers' do.'

'Right. My name's Len Rossman.'

He waved his right hand, with open fingers, rapidly from side to side.

'You'll always be Thug to me.' He laughed, so did I. 'You like music, Thug?'

I wanted to say something witty, wanted to show I could be good company, an entertaining friend, tried to think up instant nicknames for him and they ran rapidly through my head as I rejected each name – the Giraffe with a Razor, Long Day's Journey Into Space, The Dark Tower, The Best-Dressed Scaffold, The Hitchcock of Notre Dame – none of them seemed funny enough or right enough, but there was a feeling that I must, sooner or later, invent a name for him. As I struggled to say something, he rocked his long head backwards and forwards.

I said: 'You're obviously a pop star, the way you move.'

'Not a pop star. Not a musician, except sometimes. Not a musician. I'm music, that's what I am. Music and words. I sit down at a piano, any piano, and I put my fingers on those white things and I open my mouth. And – zoom, zoom, zoom, zoom, zoom – music and words come out. They make me up as I go along.'

'You're one of the Bog Spielers.'

'That remains to be heard, Thug.'

He gripped me by the shoulders for a second, crouched to the floor, said: 'Bang!' sprinted across the floor, took a leap, bent his knees, straightened them again and there he stood on the bandstand, waving as if he was on a ship leaving harbour for some war in a film. He walked round the piano, checking its breeding, its flanks, its hocks, its full complement of teeth. Then he sat down on the stool, flapped his hands above his head for a full four seconds, swung the mike around to a position about five inches from his lips and began to make – music? fun? trouble? I couldn't define it, but he was making something. It was odd, especially in a time of polished and clever pop, odd and sometimes rough when it wasn't very odd and very rough. He was letting his hands travel wherever they fancied on the keyboard, he seemed indifferent to them. He began to sing-chant-speak and his voice varied from line to line. Whether he was whispering or shouting there was certainty in that voice. The only suggestion of tension was in his eyes, focused continually on the mike. He was certainly making up the music, messing up the music, as he went along, but he had the words ready:

Standing with my back against the wall, that's all,
Standing with my back against the wall.
You know I've been standing with my back against
    that wall
Till my back is like wallpaper printed with a
    pattern of bricks.

And that wall is so thick,
And that wall is so long
It goes right round the world
And comes back, so that all
That I'm facing is that same old wall.

Standing with the wall against my back
And the same wall up against my front.
And for extra security
My front is back to back
With my back.

So if you creep up behind my front
My back will turn round and surprise you,
And if you try sneaking round the other way
My front will come up behind you.
So don't you think I'm winning?
O yes I think I'm winning.
Come on, you *know* that I'm winning.

Standing sort of upside-out,
Standing sort of inside-down,
Standing, that's my hobby,
Standing, kind of free standing,
Standing, nice word with a light sound about it,
Standing, 'the only position for a man',
Standing, how about you?
Standing, like Father Christmas on the edge of a
    chimney,
Standing, like a schoolboy reading porn,
Standing, ah they call me Cape Horn,
Standing, watching the people crawl by,
Standing, like the letter I,
Standing, with everything I've got
And everything you've got

Which comes to a lot,
Just standing, free-standing,
Up against that wonderful wall.

Then Finn was on his feet, taking a bow and shaking his head violently as he took it. His speech was short: 'Who's going to swim, now? Who's going to swim? I am.' I didn't want to swim but I wanted to talk to Finn. For the second time that day I was shaken, I didn't know if he'd done something good or bad, I had no weights and measures for that judgement, all I knew was that he'd done something freely out of his own head and that what he'd done had commanded every man and woman in the room. It was as if he'd issued an order and we'd all accepted it, but the order was in a foreign language so we didn't know what to do. I couldn't have reported what his words had been saying in a way which made any sense, I couldn't even have said what the feeling behind the words amounted to, but there was a feeling, more in the way he delivered the words than the words themselves, more in the freedom of his music than the chords themselves, there was a feeling all right and it had swept across the room and left me blinking. I followed him out of the room. He turned. His eyes were brighter and more kindly now.

'You want to swim, Thug?'

'Sure. I swim.'

'You mean you can float all that tonnage? Your bones must be made of fibreglass.'

The green-eyed girl from Purley, Surrey, joined us. Her body was all right and Purley, Surrey, is all right too, a nice place with nice people, detached, semi-detached, anyone-for-tennis at the nineteenth hole, super-tax goodtime but not my nest. At the moment I simply wanted to talk with a BG.

'Finn,' she said, 'I'd think your oversize hands and feet would sink to the bottom like four anchors.'

' "Your pedal extremities are colossal," ' he sang. 'That's Fats Waller. Quote from *Your Feet's Too Big*.'

I said: 'You're not only a musical prodigy, Mr Murdoch, you're a *scholastic genius*!' I pronounced it as if it came from one of those talk bubbles in comic books. They both recognized the style and appreciated it.

'Which beach do we invade tonight?' Finn asked.

'Drive you there,' she said. 'You too,' she said to me. 'My name's Annie Beauvais if you want to know the truth, half-French, the lower half, get yourself a towel and we'll meet by the entrance.'

Ten minutes later the three of us were crammed into a Fiat with an open top, Annie smiling to herself at the wheel, me crammed in beside her slightly bewildered at the thought of a half-French girl in Purley, my head back and my eyes gaping at the stars, Finn in the back, noisy and somehow folded into that crabbed space, but occasionally unfolding, standing up as best he could and singing a few words:

'Friends, friends,
Wherever the boulevard bends,
Everywhere I go I see friends.

'Mates, mates,
All over the bloody place,
Every face in the crowd belongs to a mate.'

After computerizing the rhythm and the rhymes, I mentally rejected a couple of verses, then found one and sang back at him:

'Chums, chums,
Whatever the world becomes,
Its entire population consists of chums.'

Annie joined in the game:

'Pals, pals,
Men, women, children and even animals,
The whole solar system is full of my pals.'

We laughed, a laughter trio. Finn broke off in mid-guffaw. He leaned forward between us and said, very seriously and urgently:

'I think we've stumbled across something very important, I think we're stumbling very well tonight. No, I mean it. That song. Yes? We just made it together. Yes? Well, if you think about it, if you really sit down and think about it, well you are sitting down, good, yeah, if you think about it now – it's the absolute opposite, the total opposite of Old Man Paranoia. And you know it's paranoia that stops the world going round when it should be revolving on its axis, revolving, revolving. No, look – everyone goes round afraid of other people, all the time, some of them bluster it out, some of them think they're just shy, but they're all being eaten up, eaten up alive, eaten up half-alive by paranoia fish. If you put your hand into a bowl of paranoia fish they will strip it down to your skeleton, down to the five finger bones, within five minutes. That's if you keep it in the bowl for five minutes. Scientific fact.'

Finn took his left hand in his right and examined it very carefully for signs of nibbling. Annie said cheerfully:

'Know what you mean, Finn. But paranoia is when you're suspicious and afraid of other people for no reason at all. But all the people you're talking about, and I'm one of them and you're one of them, those people who go around afraid of other people, they've got real reasons for being afraid. They've had experience of other people who want to wound or smother or kill them any old how. So there's no paranoia about it.'

'Oh,' said Finn. Then he pulled out a bottle, unscrewed the top, took a swig and passed it over to me. 'What a beautiful theory. If the truth *is* beautiful, it's a shining theory and besides, besides, you're diminishing the good, goofy significance of our famous friendship song. Listen, I'm not afraid of you, Annie, hardly afraid of you at all. But Thug here, I don't know. Bit afraid of him, aren't you?' That question was addressed to his own belly. 'Yes, I thought so, still a bit afraid of old Thug.'

I grinned and took a swallow from the bottle. It said it was brandy on the label, but it was a new one on me, oily and slightly hot, especially when it got down inside. It made you conscious of tubes inside you which are normally without sensation.

I said: 'I'm not trying to boast. Maybe it's just that I've had an easy time, being big. But I've been thinking about people and I can't think of any of them I'm afraid of.' I didn't add – now that my father's dead. I passed the bottle to Annie, who sipped, then passed it back without looking. Finn took it, then leaned forward and ruffled my hair.

'Young,' he said. 'Young, young, young, young.'

Between rocks and ragged trees, we reached a half-moon of sand. The sea was dark jelly. We stripped off, throwing our clothes into the same heap. My excitement came partly from the brandy, partly from the shadows of Annie's body, partly from the nearness of the sea and partly from some other happiness I couldn't identify. We each took one of Annie's hands and ran to the water, she broke away from us, swam out to a rock and sat there, laughing at us and combing her hair with her fingers.

I said to Finn: 'I'll catch her when she swims back.' It was just my joke.

'Ah,' he said. 'Good idea.' He shouted to Annie. 'There's a game. You've got to try to swim to the shore without us catching you.'

'Funny game,' shouted Annie.

'You bet,' said Finn. 'Very intellectual game. And good training for all of us.'

That moment Annie stood, shining for a second, then dived. Her head didn't bob up.

'Can't have bashed that pretty head,' said Finn.

'Swimming underwater.'

'Get over that way,' he said.

We both moved a couple of yards to the left. Annie surfaced exactly between us and both of us dived at her. We stood there for some time, up to our thighs in water, her body sandwiched between our bodies. She laughed as my person rose against her, we all laughed a little, then we were standing there again without laughing. She slid down between us, and for a moment she squatted in the water, my person in one hand, Finn's in the other, then she pulled hard, pulling us together and made a dash for the beach. We pushed each other, Finn fell backwards, then we were sprinting after her. In ankle-deep water Finn Rugby tackled me and my face hit dry sand. I just laughed, it seemed to be a night for laughing and each laugh was different. My headache was back, I could feel its beat in my head. When I reached Finn and Annie they were sitting side by side, at the brandy. Annie took my hand and placed it on her thigh. Finn was in charge of her breasts.

Finn said: 'We'd better have a duel for you, Annie.'

'You'd better bloody not,' she said, 'I want you both in one piece, I mean each in one piece.'

'I'd mash him,' I said.

'You wouldn't. Finn's been through Hollow Hill. They're taught to fight with both hands tied behind their backs and their feet in solid cement. He could knock you down and truss you up with only his cock and his teeth. Never mind, baby Thug. Just let me put my head in your lap.'

My person became lost in the sopping curves of her hair. I stroked her ears and cheeks while Finn fucked her. Once I filled my mouth with brandy, leaned down and kissed her, spitting the brandy into her mouth so that she bucked and spluttered. Then Finn fell away and she turned to me. She was savage and tight around me and it was soon over. Afterwards we all went in the sea again, but this time solemnly, with no laughter at all.

I smiled as we dried ourselves, but I don't know how I smiled. An hour before I had been happier than I had ever been. Now I was full of tigers. Finn and Annie. Between them they had put me in my place. The lad, the muscle kid with plenty to learn, the lad, give him a hand-out, the lad, can't fight the six-foot-five freak because he hasn't graduated, he's not an Old Boy, never went to the grand old school at Hollow Hill. I came inside her because my glands were stimulated. As I came I wished her Josie's fate, whatever that was. And Finn, who seemed to be everything I wanted to be when I first met him, who had combined with all that professionalism a wild gaiety which I knew I could share even if I couldn't generate it myself – I could still respect his skill, but I had to despise his fears, especially his fear of me. Earlier that evening I had thought that the rest of my holiday would glide so well, cross-questioning Finn about his trade, learning how I could become a bodyguard. Now there was nothing I wanted to ask him. I knew I could be better than him.

In the car back to Port Light I deliberately chose the back seat and pretended to sleep. All the way back I was working it out. I decided not to tell them anything of what I felt. Much better if they regarded me as a friend while I recognized them as enemies. That gave me, if ever we met in future, a tremendous strategic advantage. But I'm not an actor, and the idea of pretending to be cheerful and maybe playing sex games with them was out of the question. I thought about my life as a boy and my time as a Yellow. When I thought about those times I thought of myself as three-dimensional, in full colour, in the foreground. Other people were two-dimensional, black-and-white, coming and going but usually absent altogether. I could see myself, large and solid, in a good desert, alone. I can see that picture now, at this moment. I can understand this picture. It becomes clearer. I am sitting in this desert. I am wearing ordinary street clothes. I can't see water or food or even shade anywhere in the desert. I feel no need of them. The two-dimensional people have disappeared. I am sitting absolutely still, except for the fact that I am growing bigger. Nothing is wrong. My form, my mass is filling the whole frame of the picture. I think the growing is stopping. Yes, the growing has stopped. Yes. Now I'm, you know, an inhabitant of the inside of my own head. I am walking in there. Above me there is a great curving sky of bone, a bone dome. I am walking under the sky of my skull, walking on the surface of the good desert. It's changing. Suddenly it's changing. Just then all the atoms of the air changed suddenly, they had been widely spaced and slow-moving, but just then they became sharp and whizzing, dark specks, visible, dangerous atoms. As I watch myself, the self I am watching stands up. There are buildings towering behind it, traffic criss-crossing in front of it, crowds packing around it. There is tense music. The buildings keep changing shape and place. In one of a thousand windows the dot of a head appears. The self I am watching turns on one foot, fires, and the dot has gone. Now there's something else. Yes, that car, one car in the length of a hundred-mile motorway, one car gives off the smell of an assassin. This time the self I am watching doesn't even turn to it. I concentrate my will on that car's destruction and within one second it veers off the road, smashes through a yellow barrier, down a steep bank, rolls over three times, jams into a ditch and all at once it is the buckling heart of a bulge of flame. A bugle of flame. I listen to the flame. The city is going away now. The atoms are calming down. The atoms were wolves just now, random wolves. Now the atoms are turning into a close, quiet flock of miniature sheep. I can see myself. I am in the good desert.

Yesterday you were telling me about your holiday. You were on your way back to the hotel with Annie and Finn.

Yeah, that's right. Yes, well I told you I felt bad in the car. Annie and Finn spent the night together. They asked me to join them but I flapped my right arm, pretending to be hopelessly drunk. Next morning I made the only move I had to make to keep them away. I went over to the table where they sat at coffee and told them that I'd just heard that my father had died in a road accident. I made it happen on a motorway. I said I hoped they understood, but I meant to spend the rest of my holiday thinking, planning, reading, writing letters. I said:

'You know, I just want to be entirely alone.'

I didn't wait for their sympathy, just walked away. Of course it was impossible not to glimpse them during the rest of my holiday. I kept coming across them fooling about on bicycles, boozing by the harbour or giggling in the dining-hall, but when that happened I'd just screw my eyes up, shake my head and walk on. I wrote to Yellow HQ and asked for a transfer to Hollow Hill.

Transfer had to be approved by Yellow HQ as well as the Hill, so after the standard exchange of documents I was called to HQ for an interview. It was carried out in typical we-don't-give-a-shit-for-you Yellow style. I was dumped on the bare bench of a magazineless waiting-room. Then I wasn't called for two hours, no apologies, no explanations. It wasn't a bureaucracy hang-up, it was just a Yellow tradition – if it's not urgent, keep them waiting a couple of hours. And watch them waiting through the one-way mirror. I expected all this, so I sat down, took a book about fishing out of my pocket and read it. I concentrated less on the words than on sitting in a relaxed but alert manner, just in case they were watching, and censoring any gestures, like nose-picking or face-scratching, which could be interpreted as nervous. Eventually I was summoned to an office with a burly Yellow sergeant in shirtsleeves, black hair sprouting out of his open neck, a Yellow Major, young for his rank, thin mouth, and, half hidden behind a very expensive electric typewriter, an apparent civilian. They put me in a chair, the sergeant yawned and scratched under his arms as the major, tapping delicate fingers on his glass-topped desk, put formal questions in a tone of total boredom:

'Why do you want to leave? Why do you want to be a BG? What makes you think you'd make a good BG? Do you suffer from any nervous complaints? Which television programmes do you watch?' etc, etc.

And I trotted out, clippety-clop, clickety-click, the correct answers to the time-honoured ritual riddles. Finally the major shrugged:

'Clear with us,' he said. 'Your witness, sir.'

The man in civilian clothes rose from behind the typewriter. Suddenly he was important to me. He rubbed his hand over longish, brown but greying hair and put his head on one side. He walked over to me and, just by watching the way he touched his hair, adjusted his head and walked, I could tell that (*a*) his authority was large and (*b*) he was in favour of me.

'I'm Colonel Forrest, deputy at Hollow Hill,' he said. 'We've been through your record. We like you. We'll be glad to have you at the Hill.'

He took my hand to shake it and held on to it tight.

'There's only one other thing I wanted to ask you,' he said. 'Why did you lie to Finn and Annie about your father being killed?'

As soon as he'd received the reaction from my hand, he let it drop.

'All right,' he said. 'You can tell me in the car.'

As his chauffeur drove us westwards I tried to explain, leaving out the compulsory sex, leaving out the hatred which followed the sex and making out that I'd split from Finn and Annie because I didn't trust the girl, that she seemed to me part-subvert at least. Colonel Forrest then gave me a slap-by-tickle description of the bathing incident and asked if I'd forgotten it. I said no, I remembered it, but the incident had nothing to do with my lie to Finn and Annie. If I didn't trust Annie, he asked, why hadn't I warned Finn? Come to that, why hadn't I informed the chainwork? I said, because I had no tangible evidence, it was only intuition and the whole style of the girl. I said I didn't think an aura was any use as Exhibit A. He asked if I didn't think it my duty to investigate any suspicions I might have, however flimsy? Was I afraid that the girl might pump me? All through this question-and-answer pursuit he never once shattered my feeling that he was on my side, that he wanted me to be able to answer him. But finally I was cornered.

I said: 'Look, it was the first holiday I'd ever had in my life and I wanted it to be a real holiday, a real rest. I didn't want to spend it interrogating a girl just on the basis of a Holmesy hunch, did I? I was tired.'

He said: 'Yes, you were tired, weren't you? You cried.'

My only accurate preconceptions about Hollow Hill were that it was in Wiltshire, that it ran a tough course, and that I would like it very much indeed. If there were suicides, I never saw them. There could have been. The whole place was designed to test your balance. Many must have toppled. A hard place, its nature was split and it was likely to split you.

At Hollow Hill, no two men go through the same programme. You never know what will happen the next day or which part of the course you will be assigned to, whether you will sleep in a chromium suite in the Jacobean mansion at the head of Hollow Hill Park, in its mouse-ridden attics, down the park in a crowded, fart-filled billet, or even farther down in a wooden stable in a continuous crossfire of draughts. You may suddenly find yourself flown to some foreign city, some President about to swoop in, with only two hours in which to find the men who'll brief you, collect your briefing, get to your post and stick there till relieved by someone with the right documents. Nobody usually tells you if you've done a job well or badly. Your pay varies from week to week and sometimes even your payday varies. Orders may conflict. One day you may be given a personal order to spend the next twelve hours contemplating in silence and learning by heart the mechanisms of various firearms, but you have to perform this while you're carrying out other orders – to cook, to thunder round the combat course, or swim to the point of exhaustion while discussing security wrinkles with other swimmers. Another trainee may have been instructed to attack and disable (without maiming) as many other trainees as possible without being caught. Yet another may be playing the role of a subvert, attempting to spread disaffection, again without being reported. No wonder trainees crack.

They say that Hollow Hill never turns out two identical BGs. You see the point of that – normally BGs work in teams, so it's best if each man is a specialist. The incentive is simply this – that if you can emerge from the training machine as a man rather than as Shredded Wheat, you win a small card in a black leather case. All the men are volunteers, hand-picked and mainly ex-Yellow. The only threat necessary is the threat of failure.

Despite the anti-routine structure of the courses, there's no common factor in everyone's training at the Hill. Know your enemy takes almost as much time in the schedule as know your job. There are lectures, films and books on revolutionary theory, not just the popular versions, the real hard stuff. Plus the questioning, with reasonable restraints, of certain selected genuine political criminals. Trainees have to play the parts of subverts, engaging in plots which usually follow some pattern of arson, sabotage or, most commonly, assassination. If you didn't know the Hill's true end, you might have taken it for an Assassins' College. We studied the great bumpings – Ferdinand, the Kennedys and Trotsky, etc. We studied the character-prints of their assassins, their motives, their weapons, their strategy, their timing. We worked out BG security patterns and how they could be pierced. We were encouraged to invent assassination fantasies – the comic-smear assassination in which a lavatory cistern explodes, killing the two occupants of the cubicle, a distinguished statesman *and a friend*. The ideal assassination. The ideal target. Group assassination. The choice of a deputy or vice-president as a deterrent to assassination. Weighing up the results of a sane assassination. Assassinating a member of your own side in order to rouse public opinion against the other side. The assassination of ostensibly non-political figures – film stars, gang leaders, astronauts – we were forced to brood on the subject until it dominated our dreams.

It was in my fourth week that I wrote in my diary: 'If I'm to be a bodyguard, I will be the best bodyguard in the world. This morning, as dawn was breaking out, I woke pleased. I had been dreaming that I was a bodyguard.' Ten minutes later I was not so happy. I was taken for a forty-eight-hour interrogation. A great many of the questions were about my father. I suppose I didn't do badly, for I was allowed twelve hours' sleep afterwards.

Throughout the chaos of my days at Hollow Hill, there was one recurring factor – the man who controlled the place. It wasn't that you saw him every day, in his dark-red uniform, but the name Commander Gray was penned at the end of every printed order and was used as a final authority in lecture after lecture. He would appear silently in doorways, his thin face relaxed, cool eyes wide open as if in surprise, silver hair roughly brushed, with the air of a ghostly statesman. You received a sense that inside him was a centre of raging force which would only erupt in the most extreme emergency. Among many physically bigger men, he seemed by far the strongest, the least vulnerable. I was still susceptible to the magic of rank at that time, but it had very little to do with my feelings about the commander. From his men he conjured devotion. He was the perfect image of authority. No other man I have ever worked with impressed me so much, though in every one of them I have searched for some hint of the commander's inner power. One evening, just before dinner, he sent for me. His flat was splashed with dark, tropical colours. A calm girl in a white dress moved past a tank of illuminated fish the size of pennies. She brought us whiskies. I'd never heard the commander speak before and I was jolted by the way his husky voice jerked from sentence to sentence, very quietly, very insistently.

'Rossman. You're doing well. Would've been shocked if you hadn't. You're explosive, Rossman, I think explosive is the word, but your time-bomb's in the right place. How are your headaches?'

'Mild, sir. I'm too busy to bother with them.'

'If I understand you well, Rossman, Hollow Hill must be purgatory for you, a purgatory you welcome because it leads up through the pearly gates and slap, bang into the middle of the heavenly host of bodyguards. I see I do understand you pretty well. If the future had a colour, Rossman, what colour would it be?'

His voice had been rocking me to sleep. I tried to think fast, but black was the first colour which seeped into my head and I knew that wasn't right so I blinked both eyes and forced another picture.

'Bright yellow,' I said. 'Same colour as the sun.'

'Right, the sun's shining down. Like a circular riot policeman. Yellow sun, yellow sun. What's it shining down on?'

'Well, a desert, sir,' I said. I could see that desert.

'And do you like it?'

'Yes.'

'What's in the desert?'

'Sand with rocks which have got holes worn in them by the sand.'

'Anything moving in the desert?'

'Yes, there's a man. Me.'

'Yes. You'll do, Rossman. At least you don't repeat my questions.'

'I'll do for what, sir?'

'Tomorrow's exercise. I'll be giving a spiel, in the big lecture hall at two in the afternoon. You'll try to bump me with this. Fires six red-dye pellets.'

He handed me a ridiculous air pistol and a cardboard box which rattled in my hand.

'Does anyone know I'll be trying, sir?'

'You'll all be warned there's going to be an attempt. They won't know who. But the warning goes out in two hours. That gives you a slight start over security.'

When you take a pet dog into a strange house, it wants to explore the entire building and the surrounding grounds, mapping out the place in terms of smell, before it chooses a warm place in the room where the humans are, turns around twice and lies down contentedly. Happily, I share this instinct. Since my arrival at Hollow Hill I'd spent my spare time surveying the intricate, sometimes apparently random, layout of the place, memorizing which doors were usually locked, which windows were barred, which offices had external telephones, the places where prowlers, motor-bikes and bicycles were parked and where each line of the tarmac cobweb of paths might lead. All this knowledge, in itself, might have been useless, but I was training myself as hard as they were training me, I wanted to push my brain to the point where it could record information, especially environmental information, with casual accuracy. This private course was already paying off. I could recite the position, shape, main features, approaches and exits of the big lecture hall without a pause. As I walked to the hall to exploit my two hours' start, I ran the facts through my brain.

The hall, usually reserved for special events, is on the second floor of a T-shaped building, about half a mile from the entrance to the camp and about two hundred yards from an easily penetrated perimeter fence. That fence is twelve feet high, several years old, not very strong and topped with one strand of ordinary barbed wire. Between the building and the fence are the gymnasium and then the football pitch. Ground floor of the T-shaped building – mainly offices, occupied 9–5, barred windows. First floor of the T-shaped building – study rooms and library, no bars on the windows, two staircases but no corridors, just inter-connecting rooms locked only at night. Second floor of the T-shaped building – at one end, the top of the T, a few study rooms behind the stage of the lecture hall. Two doors from study rooms lead to the back of the stage, but the hall is usually reached by a wide wooden staircase, highly polished, with two entrances through swing doors. A long hall, full of light from high windows adjustable by dangling cords, the floor yellow with constant waxings, the steel-framed chairs shining in their rows. But that day the stage was the most significant feature: an old-fashioned piece of woodwork, proscenium arch with curtains at the front, curtains at the back, a lighting gallery, one trapdoor at the front and a longer trapdoor behind the back curtains. I knew all this before I started work. After an hour I'd done enough, or as much as I could do in safety. I went to the canteen and was sucking at a Coke with an ice-cream float when the assassination attempt was announced in advance over the speakers. Somebody stopped the jukebox. I took notes along with the other trainees.

I could only sleep for about two hours that night It was so funny, having to pretend to kill the man I most admired in the world in order to prove my value to him. And funny became disquieting as I began to think myself deeper and deeper into the assassin's role, as I imagined myself, seeing the picture as clearly as I could, raising the pistol to shoot him. I had to run the whole exercise through again and again. After doing this six times, trying to account for every possible mistake, I ran it through again, this time as if it were no exercise, but a real assassination. This was hard at first, the pictures in my head became blurred, the colour tended to run out of them, the ache began to grip. I tried harder, clenching my forehead like you do when the mental going is rough. All my prejudices were against a clear run, something was bound to crap me up. I tried to imagine that Commander Gray was actually a member of The Rot, but this meant figuring out how he had evaded the chain-work throughout his career, no, it meant more than that, it meant changing his face. Whenever I tried to superimpose another face, Gray-like but with the marks of The Rot, it became absurd, the whole film turned into a cartoon. It was more possible, and, I told myself, more relevant, to imagine myself as part of The Rot. To short-cut the daydream process – and I take daydreams seriously as a working method – I postulated that I had been a perfectly law-abiding citizen until my sister (whom I imagined rapidly as the Revenge student Josie) had been arrested and had died under Yellow interrogation. The order for her arrest had come from the commander. I was happier when I'd established this, and I went through the scenario twice, once slowly, once fast. Then I looked at it as a movie, ran it through, stopping at various key frames and analysing the possibilities. Nothing would go exactly as planned; that was about the only thing I could bet on. But for every danger I tried to work out a counter-move. I managed to whittle away some of the bad chances. It was important to be flexible, I must be ready to recognize and grab any good chance which flew my way.

Next morning I was with the group on weapon training. My aim was only average, lack of sleep and a tension in my neck set up a tremor in my hands which I could feel even if it wasn't visible. But everything you do at the Hill counts towards your final rating, so I tried to forget the looming afternoon, wiped the coating of sweat from my hands, took a new grip on my supersten and began to score well. Second part of the morning was Political Education (Historical) and I caught myself becoming over-aggressive as our group discussed the subvert movements, such as they were, of the 'fifties and 'sixties, pushing for the view that even genteel forms of protest had been very dangerous because they tended to erode general confidence. I think I made a poor impression. Colonel Forrest listened to me patiently and pointed out that I was making the mistake of applying present-day standards of security to a different situation. In the sixties it had been impossible, he said, to suppress all signs of subversion. Public opinion was still too confused about security, and censorship had been turned, temporarily, into a dirty word by prolonged intellectual campaigns. So successive governments attempted to contain the often vague discontents of the time.

After lunch the real business began. At 1.30 precisely the doors were unlocked and the trainees were allowed into the lecture hall, two hundred of us, joking our way up those wide stairs, shouldering each other in our eagerness to outwit the assassin. We swarmed about, checking that only two outside windows overlooked the stage, sending two men to check that the rooms behind those windows were locked, making sure that the mike was wired without booby traps, moving the chairs farther from the stage, placing a small reading podium on the stage table so that the commander would present a slightly smaller target, reading a roll-call of all trainees so we could be sure that none was lurking on the roof, watching each other out of the corner of our eyes, hamming up the whole dramatic situation. By 1.45 they'd found, as I intended, one of the improvised smoke bombs I'd rigged up in the lighting gallery, apparently timed to spring at 2.20. This went into a bucket of water. Then another was spotted, dangling high above the stage from a rope, but impossible to reach without a ladder, which was, unfortunately for the searchers, in one of the rooms behind the stage. These rather home-made-looking bombs, which would have worked accurately enough, caused five minutes' panic and considerable concentration on the lighting gallery. They also meant that, five minutes before the commander was due to appear, the stage was crammed with trainees, most of them looking upwards. It was left to me to point out the trapdoor almost exactly under the table behind which the commander would stand. The trapdoor's hinges were on the auditorium side. I jerked it open and shouted:

'I want one man to come down here and search under the stage. No room for a crowd. One man, quick, let's have you. We'll stay down here during the speech in case anyone tries anything.'

I'd rehearsed the right words and, even if they did sound artificial, they worked. I was joined under the stage by a big trainee with freckles all over his flattened nose. He had no light, but I carried a box of matches. There was a faint smell of sick down there, I might have imagined it, but with two hundred aggressively-oriented trainees you can't help a few violent incidents. By the flare of matches we found nothing but old stage props, a stag's head decorated with blue mould, wooden stools and several boxes strewn around to form a miniature maze. Privately I discovered something new, however, a small round beam of light piercing the front of the stage. I made a note of that. The two of us moved around bent double.

'Hey,' he said. 'There's another trapdoor at the back of the stage.'

'Shut up, he's starting to speak.'

I could hear Commander Gray clearly enough. The PA system was pure. He was talking about concentration.

'... and of course we want you to be superhuman, otherwise there'd be no point in this place. We want you to develop faculties which most men have never used. When you're guarding a target, enlarge your concentration. That concentration should be intense and complex enough to take in several pieces of information simultaneously. Attempt this, starting now, while you're guarding me. Part of that concentration must be upon me, where I'm standing, whether I shift my position slightly like this and for a second or two offer a larger area of myself to the gun, whether my voice falters as if I'm being affected by some gas or poison, whether I suddenly say something which might provoke an uncertain assassin. We are dancing-partners. I lead, you follow. Right. Now let that part of your concentration stay with me. The rest of your concentration must be subdivided. You must be aware of any movement in the hall, no matter whose movement it is; your eyes must take in gradual movements as well as sudden ones. Your ears must be listening for anything. A change in the note of the central heating may be a deadly warning. A shadow on the floor. A member of the audience scratching his head...'

I listened to the words, but not only to the words. I was also listening to the occasional scuffing of the commander's feet a few inches behind the trap. The freckled man lurched over and crouched beside me. At that moment I realized how to use that circle of light in the front of the stage. Through a hole the size of a thumbnail I looked and saw Colonel Forrest, arms folded, sitting in the front row. I whispered to Freckles:

'You'd better be ready under the trapdoor at the back.'

He put one hand on my shoulder in agreement, I lit a match for him and he stumbled back there. I don't know why he obeyed me, I had arguments ready for him, but he just took my orders. Now the commander had changed gear. He was assuring the audience that, simply by attending Hollow Hill, their names would certainly appear on The Rot's death list of elements to be destroyed after a revolution. How seriously did we take this revolution? Well, we had better take it as seriously as we took our own lives from now on.

I stood directly between Freckles and the round hole. I drew my air pistol furtively, which is an adverb I like, brought its snub muzzle up to the thumbnail hole, aimed, pulled, and the pellet splattered redness all over Major Forrest's chest. He wiped at the dye with his left hand and looked up at the stage in surprise, standing up. Uproar.

'Stay back there,' I shouted to Freckles. 'I'll see what's up.'

I pushed open the trap above my head. The commander was like a crimson tower on the verge of my trench. As he stared down I could see the hairs in his nostrils as I fired twice, point blank, chest and face, the red dye spreading as I ducked down.

'Get over here,' I shouted. 'He's been hit.'

Freckles crouched his way over, but at the last minute I moved to one side, pulling his arm and tripping him so that he fell under the heels of two BGs as they jumped down the trap together. While they untangled themselves I was pushing open the back trapdoor, running behind the back-stage curtains, scooting through a study room and down the stairs to the first floor. From there I had an obstacle course through study rooms and the library until I gained the base of the T-shaped building. The library window was still open, as I'd left it. I vaulted through it and into the librarian's car, a tough little Renault. He always left the key in it. A siren screamed behind me. I swerved around the gym, which gave me adequate cover as I zagged across the football pitch and through the fence at the point where I'd weakened it beforehand. I kept the Renault on its feet past some trees and braked sharply when I reached a deep ditch. I jumped the ditch and stood on the main road, hitching with every appearance of calm and getting picked up within a minute. I got off at Salisbury, where I went to a cinema and then phoned the camp. I'd been lucky. They told me later that the boys who grabbed Freckles yelled: 'We've got him.' That helped. Freckles didn't know my name, and since there were BGs in the lighting gallery, on the stairs, on the roof and everywhere by that time, it took some minutes before they realized that Rossman was a bit too missing to be true. When I returned to the Hill I was taken to see Commander Gray. His comment was very simple. He laughed.

I knew that the whole exercise had been, in certain ways, schoolboyish, over-complicated and too reliant on good luck, but I was still proud of it. It had worked. And the diversion of shooting Colonel Forrest, which certainly distracted a good percentage of that famous concentration, was entirely due to my noticing that hole at the last moment, an unplanned manoeuvre which just jumped out of my head. The next day I had to explain the whole exercise, from my own point of view, in the same hall. I was reluctant to do that, for it seemed important to me, at that time, not to let other people know how my mind worked.

When I finished speaking a trainee with a thin voice asked if I hadn't relied too strongly on diversionary tactics. It seemed to me a weak-kneed criticism, but I didn't have to consider it. Commander Gray curtailed question time.

He said: 'You lot had better learn from this. Rossman's mission was simply to assassinate me. He wasn't even asked to assassinate me and make a getaway. Assassins don't expect to get away. But you let him bump Colonel Forrest, then bump me and then make a clean break out of camp and over the horizon. Four of you should have been under the stage and another three in each of the rooms behind the stage. But Rossman knew damn well he was working against pretty primitive, amateur security conditions and he used that knowledge. He even used that "I am the boss" voice to persuade you that only two men were needed under the stage. I want the rest of you to think about what he did. Work out exactly how he did it.'

He spoke quickly and coldly. When he'd finished he walked out of the hall, leaving me with a great deal of prestige and no popularity at all. Two months later I left the Hill, my certificate neatly folded in an inside pocket.

Although the Hill's run by the State, the passed-out BG is lucky if he's assigned to a Stateroll job right away – many BGs have to practise privately when they start, and although there can be rich pickings in this sector, with the chairmen of major companies for example, such jobs don't form part of the ladder which leads to the top, for the top, in my opinion, must be the assignment of guarding either the Prime Minister or a member of the Royal Family. That's where I was aiming.

I'm not much given to regret, which seems to me one of the many emotions which a man should rub along without. But if I'd foreseen the hypertension and ultimately the farce ahead, I would gladly have avoided my first real BG assignment. But it was a national interest job, Whitehall-commissioned, and, especially when your certificate's not dry, you don't argue with Stateroll.

The phone rang as I stood, half-soaped and half-soaked, in the shower of my cupboard-like London flat, scrubbing away the minute grit and musky sweat of another day's work waiting for work. I strode out of the shower and, dripping profusely over the telephone directories, picked up the receiver. Unfortunately the combination of my wetness and faulty equipment supplied by the GPO meant that during the conversation which followed I was subject to a series of small and irritating electric shocks, as if someone was caressing me with nettles. Looking back on them, they could have been some kind of warning, if I believed in that sort of thing, but I don't. Maybe I surprised the telephonist by my impatience. It was a full seven minutes before I received my instructions – pack a suitcase and take a taxi to the Ministry of Education. By this time the soaped parts of my torso had dried to form an itching crust. The small electric shocks continued.

'But how long's the assignment for?' I asked.

'Not long. Don't worry. Everything will be taken care of. Only a couple of weeks or so. I'm sure you'll enjoy it. What do you look like?'

It was bloody unprofessional. The secretary at the other end of the phone began to giggle and exchange indecipherable jibes with a vague male voice, an interruption which lasted at least another minute, while I began to shiver, since my bedroom window was, as usual, wide open for reasons of health. At last the girl returned her attention to me and I was able to say an abrupt goodbye, hang up the stinging receiver, wash the cracking skin of soap off my body under the shower (which was now running cold) dress and pack hurriedly.

As I entered the tall grey hallway of the Ministry, a voice rang out, somewhat obscured by echoes. It was the voice of a man who is accustomed to obedience from fools.

'Are you the new BG? Where've you been, you double-barrelled craphound? I've been standing here – not sitting you'll notice – standing here on my varicose legs, shoes squeezing my feet to death – standing here swaying in the draught for ten minutes, twelve minutes precisely. You can see that I'm standing up, can't you? You've observed that? And if you peer a little closer you'll see that I'm not in any kind of a youth movement either. And you can also probably guess by now that I'm not the sort of man who enjoys hanging about being a clothes-hanger, especially in hallways full of bad breath. Or are you as thick as you look?'

The voice came from a shortish old man with hair the colour of aluminium. I recognized him as General 'Patch' de Vere Cartwright, veteran of the unhappy African campaigns of the seventies and now Joint Minister of Education. I knew him less by his features, which were somewhat flattened though otherwise commonplace enough, than by the tropical uniform which he had idiosyncratically retained from his fighting days and by the famous patch which covered the area from which his left ear had been sliced by an African who threw an electric fan at him. I recalled him saying, in a TV interview, that the slicing had not been particularly painful, certainly not as bad as toothache. His appointment to the outer cabinet had been welcomed by the newspapers, who regarded him as a personality and certainly above party politics.

Behind the general stood Annie Beauvais, wearing an incredibly old-fashioned evening dress of candy-floss colour and texture, with a low, drooping neckline. During the general's speech she pouted at me with amusement and fanned herself with a pink shorthand notebook, glancing from time to time at the chauffeur who stood beside her, a swarthy fellow, about 6 foot 1 inch, his eyebrows colliding, eyes squeezed shut with some secret pleasure, a shiny peaked cap on the back of his head and one hand raised to his mouth, no doubt covering a smile. I was immediately unhappy. If there was anyone in the world I wanted no truck with, it was with Annie. As for the chauffeur, well, if a man's own team sniggers behind his back, security is obviously unsteady. I thought to myself: they should be prepared to die for him. All right, he may have his absurdities, but so do I, and it's not my job to look on him as a joke, but as a target to be guarded, and at this rate it looks as if I'll have to guard him against the irresponsibility of his own staff. All right, I'm prepared to do that, and not for his sake but mine, because I take myself seriously and my job even more seriously. I am, from this moment, prepared to die for him.

As we walked to the car, the general indicated Annie and the chauffeur without looking at them:

'The woman's Miss Beauvais, my secretary, used to do top security but they dropped her in the last purge. Don't worry, it was just the usual chainwork overkill. Anyway, there's nothing top secret about me. Good girl. Knows a lot of languages, very good with her tongue, eh? The chauffeur's called Dent, stout fellow. Knows about boats. Met him on a boat in fact. What's your name again? Rossman? Scotch? Jewish? Mixture? Rossman, never mind your ancestry, you'll travel in the back with me and I'll brief you on the way. What's in that bloody great trunk, Rossman?'

'Luggage, sir. Clothes and things. Equipment.'

Annie paused on her way to the front passenger seat and stared at me with experienced eyes.

'Good to see you, Len,' she said. 'Always good to see an old friend on the way up.'

Once in the back seat the general slid the black glass which separated the driver's compartment from us until it was almost closed. If I leaned forward I could just see Dent starting the limousine while Annie, apparently, was whispering into his ear.

'Lean back, Rossman, and let me shoot you the guff.'

As the car began to move, muttering past Big Ben, the briefing began at the top of the general's voice. Immediately aware that every word could be overheard in the front of the car, I requested that the radio should be switched on. The general looked for a second as if he was on the point of striking me. Then, as I nodded several times and tilted my head to indicate Annie and Dent, he gave an enormous smile, showing some awe-inspiring teeth, and clapped me on the shoulder brusquely or briskly.

'That's right,' he shouted. 'Miss Beauvais!'

Through the narrow oblong slit at the side of the black glass she shoved her porcelain nose. The skin valley between her nostrils and her upper lip was deep and delicate.

'Turn on the radio,' said the general. 'And let's have it loud and clear, woman. Foreground music, you know.'

'Any particular programme, sir?'

The general laughed and threw a feinted punch towards her nose.

'Whatever you fancy, woman.'

'Thank you, General. I'll twiddle about till I find what I want.'

I must have grimaced, I was so surprised and, well, bored by these sexual innuendoes splashing about all over the leatherette interior. Almost instantaneously the radio opened fire, very loudly, a magazine show of some sort, with interviews, short talks or parables, comical sketches and songs in different styles, something for everyone in fact, but it made the briefing difficult to assimilate.

'Fact is, Rossman, as I daresay you know from the colour supps, my daughter's getting married, eldest daughter Lucy, and about time, she's pushing twenty-five and never been legal. They say she's well, luscious, which is beside the point or at least let's forget it for the moment. *Lots of us grow roses at home, and some of us grow prize roses, but now let's meet a man who not only grows prize roses – he eats them!* Marriage has got to go like a military operation, though not like some military operations I could mention, and this is where you come in, Rossman. We've had threats, not just to me, I'm used to threats, but threats to Lucy and her bridesmaids. A fine team of girls they are, too. *Chain me down, oh lover, chain me down. Trying to hold myself together. But my mind keeps flying apart. Got a furnace where my stomach should be. And a great big HOLE in my heart – Oh chain me down –* Let alone the presents. Now the presents are of great significance too, and my staff are keeping their eyes and ears skinned – what are you staring at Rossman? You'll soon get used to me only having one ear. Don't be embarrassed by it. I'm not embarrassed about it, am I? You look at my good ear, it's a meaningless bit of flesh stuck on to the outside of my head, see, a bit of flesh flap, you know. The hole that leads to the eardrum is the important feature. Correct? Anyway, it doesn't, as I say, embarrass me. After all, it does happen to be my ear. Or it was my ear – *I well remember the first arrest I ever made. It was midnight and I was passing Hampstead Heath, when I noticed some blobs in a tree. Well they looked like blobs at first, there was lamplight nearby. Then I realized they were faces, not blobs. There were six of them, aged about sixteen, sitting in that tree. I arrested them for sitting in that tree.* Now Lucy's a funny girl, I suppose you can say that about all my girls, or about any girl for that matter. It's certainly true about Lucy and her friends, the bridesmaids, very sweet but a funny lot. If they give you any trouble, Rossman, you'll inform me won't you? Because I want to know what's going on under my nose, you ask anyone and they'll tell you, old Patch likes to know what's going on under his nose. *For there's something in your eyes, something in your eyes.* Now you know I think these threats are originating from three separate groups – one lot after Lucy, one lot after the bridesmaids and one lot after the wedding presents. First two groups are probably political enemies of mine, though as you've heard I'm above politics, or they're above me. *I first decided to become an architect when I saw the dry-stone walls of the Yorkshire Dales, snaking away over the landscape. At that time I only wanted to build walls as amazing as those. Now, of course, I specialize in government buildings.* The service itself should be watertight. Being held in my own grounds, outdoors you know, grove of trees, got a good padre coming from the Isle of Wight, he's got his head screwed on, the right way round too. *Reginald, whatever are you doing in the deep freeze? Just looking for a snack, lover. (Laughter) At this time of night? (Laughter)* You see?'

By leaning forward occasionally, I was receiving disconcerting glimpses of the activity in the front of the car. Dent's hand, sleekly gloved in yellow leather, appeared on Annie's knee. Annie, with both hands, was unrolling the glove from Dent's hand. By now it was dark, and all this was seen in flashes as we passed through the sulphur-coloured areas under street-lamps. Suddenly the general clapped his hands, leaned forward and clasped the speaking tube.

'Time?' he demanded. I saw three hands jump apart. Dent's voice, amplified and with a pronounced North-West Mediterranean accent, spoke back.

'Eleven fifteen, sir. Did you want to make a stop?'

'Of course I want to make a stop, dammit. Next place you see. Been winding up all day, haven't I? Got to wind down somehow. Correct?'

Within two minutes we'd drawn up in the car park of a sham Victorian pub, its customers slamming, backing and lurching around in the shifting headlights. The general turned to me.

'You drink, I suppose.'

'Now and then, sir. Not on duty.'

'You'll drink with me, Rossman. Part of your duty. Orders.'

He climbed out. As we walked towards the pub I thought I'd better mention it.

'I don't think they'll serve us, sir. Past closing-time.'

Saying 'sir' gives me a faint satisfaction. It's not a fashionable word. Subverts, even when they're trying to pass, find it hard to pronounce. But it gives me an air of security, a feeling of knowing where I stand and where everyone else stands. The general raised his fist, then struck it into the palm of his other hand with stinging force. He looked at the red-splotched receiving palm, then laughed.

'Serve us? They'll be bloody grovelling to serve us, Rossman. Just watch out if you want to see a good grovel.'

As we reached the door, the landlord was locking it from inside. The general bashed on wood. An angry voice answered from inside, pitched high. The general lifted the flap of the letter-box, bending athletically to do so.

'Come on, landlord, we know you're in there. We want a drink, pronto.'

'Closing-time's eleven here.'

'Landlord,' and this time the general bellowed. 'This is the Joint Minister of Education.' Silence. 'Landlord, this is General Patch.' Silence. 'Landlord, this is General Patch de Vere Cartwright and, as far as I'm concerned, closing-time is opening-time.'

The bolts jumped back, the door opened, lights flicked on and suddenly we were in a glowing back room, the general was beaming from a deep chair of scarlet leather and a silver pint tankard appeared in front of him, soon to be joined by a dozen bottles of whisky, different brands from the almost white to the golden-brown. The landlord, fat but pale, bent over us. He murmured:

'A great privilege ... living legend ... honoured ...'

'Never mind all that. Give my BG something too. What'll it be, Rossman?'

He said it as if giving a signal to relax. I tried to accept the benevolence he was trying to exude.

'Same as you, General, if that's all right.'

'You're a sport, Rossman, or you're an ignoramus. Right, landlord, fill the flowing et cetera. Tankard for Rossman.'

Two tankards stood side by side, waiting. The general squinnied at the whisky bottles, finally choosing four. Then he blended them in the tankards until we were confronted by a pint of whisky each, including a good percentage of old malt whisky.

'I'm an ignoramus, sir, I couldn't survive all that.'

'I'll use what you can't, Rossman,' he said, gulping. I sipped. It tasted explosive. By the time I'd drunk half an inch, the general's tankard was half empty. Soon after that he was looking at me through its amber-smeared glass base. I nodded and poured most of my drink slowly into his tankard, one eyebrow raised. He never said 'when'. His second tankard vanished more slowly and as he drank he talked, words tumbling now, speech getting faster and faster, taking the corners on two wheels.

'Rossman, I agree with you. From this great height I look down and I hear what you say and I tell you that I agree with you. I never drink on duty either. Never drink in the day, it gives me a dry sort of pain not drinking at lunch time, but it's a pain I can bear, I quite like it. I save it up all day, all that thirst, I keep it coiled up inside my gut, like a snake turning into dust. But when I've finished staring out my superiors, or shouting down my inferiors, when I'm homeward bound, when I've earned some sleep, then, Rossman, I hit it. I hit it.

'That name of yours Rossman, that's a good name, "Rossman", tough, two-square, two legs, two shoulders, two balls – "Ross" – sounds like the name of a rock off the coast of Scotland, or is it part of Scotland, it sounds rocky anyway, on this rock I shall build my, er, rock. And – "man" – well that's man, I suppose, man standing alone, his legs apart, strong, impregnable, impregnable-sounding name, man stand apart on that rock in the Scottish ocean. Fine soldiers, Scots. Good name. No, but when I drink I need a real drink. Hate pills, don't understand how they work. I believe they take the threads of your nerves and tie knots in them. All really poison really all those pills, little doses for little deaths, that's all they are Rossman. Hate pills, but I like sleep. And after work my head's buzzing like one of those little transformers they used to use with electric train sets, buzz, buzz, buzzing too fast, travelling you know, speeding. And I have to stop it. I can't drift into sleep like a cloud. I have to go for the knock-out.'

By the end of tankard two he was ready to be counted out. The landlord and I trundled him out to the car. There was laughter and a sigh from the front seat. The door slammed, the landlord gave a humble thumbs-up sign, the general slumped into the corner and began to snore. We began to move again.

Once, fighting against the lullaby hum of the engine, I leaned forward and peered into the front of the car. In the low glow I saw that Dent's flies were unzipped and that Annie was holding his person in her right hand. Then I noticed that Dent was glancing at me in the rear-view mirror and so I jerked backwards, but not before seeing his grin. Around twenty minutes later, Annie's face appeared. She whispered to me for a light, then half-turned away, moving from the waist, to take a cigarette from the glove shelf in front of her. I took my lighter, heavy steel, and pushed my right arm through the gap beside the dividing glass. Before I could snap her a light, the lighter was gently levered out of my fist. I left my hand there, open, waiting for the lighter to return. My hand was pushed downwards and my palm was spread over something damp, no, a little moist, very warm and soft-tipped, my hand was being pushed and pressed over the bare right breast of Annie. Erotic telegrams were tapped out, conveying shape, texture, firmness, weight and without thinking I squeezed my neck down into my shoulders, looking silly I've no doubt. I don't look for sex, there are too many complications and wounds and probably worse than that if the woman is Annie. But the pressure of sex can't be avoided completely. I'm normal enough. I felt alternate heaviness and weightlessness in my stomach, and heavy swallowing in my throat. A breast given by surprise into your hand is a rare thing. There was a pain behind my eyes, itching in my dusty tear ducts. I tensed and relaxed and tensed and relaxed that hand, although I knew that was what she expected me to do. In the centre of my palm, where two pink lines form a miniature St Andrew's Cross, her nipple pressed. I felt the shifting weight on the flesh just beside the karate edge of my hand. Carefully, but quickly, I withdrew my arm. My left hand stroked my right for comfort. I heard laughter from the front, so I laughed too, as if I meant it and they laughed back, perhaps at my laughter. An hour later we were snaking up the drive towards the general's country home, a smaller-scale Windsor Castle, flood-lit and painted pink.

At seven next morning nobody seemed to be awake, so I decided on a quick reccy. Postponing any exploration of the towers and gusty corridors, I decided to walk once around the building and then move through the surrounding parkland in an outward spiral. A bad feeling knocked inside me as I inspected the ground-floor windows – only three of them were barred. The outer walls of the castle, seen under the sun, were astounding in their pinkness. The paint was recent, as if for the wedding, and evidently lay on many previous layers of paint. It was not only too bright, it was wrong, wrong in the same way as a lipstick fired from a Luger. Real castles are grey. They look their best when the sky around them is also grey. Pink was a totally eccentric choice, not even a fashionable colour. Whoever chose the paint, whether it was the general or his daughter, was not only odd, but powerful as well in this huge household, able to override the natural objections which pink would arouse among the well-balanced element. Or perhaps there was no such element, the whole family might be asymmetrically minded, laced with eccentricity. Probably a very old family or something. It strikes me now that this insistent worry about pink paint may seem a little out of proportion to you. The point is this. Oddness in a painter or a hermit or a tramp or even a revolutionary may be an advantage for such people. But eccentricity is never socially desirable in responsible people. In a minister of the Crown it could be deadly. The pinkness of the castle only amplified the alarm I still felt from learning that the general, by his own admission, put himself to sleep each night with whisky – a small, habitual suicide. He could hardly be held responsible for the somewhat haphazard shape of the castle itself, but its pinkness was certainly his responsibility.

After an hour's walk I'd sussed out most of the park and was slightly happier, since the estate was surrounded by a ten-foot wall, spiked, with no overhanging trees. This wall was pink, too, on the inside at least, but this bothered me less. After all, it would make a good background against which to spot intruders, who were unlikely to wear pink. On my rounds of the park I gathered information which I did not fully understand. There was an artificial lake with wooden huts grouped around it. There was a dance floor protected by plastic sheeting in the centre of a wood, in some of the trees were small Tarzan houses. In fact wherever I wandered I kept encountering huts of various sizes and designs, some no more than tool-sheds, some as elaborate as scaled-down Taj Mahals. Most had their curtains drawn, but through the windows of one I observed a cocktail cabinet of thirties design, valuable stuff. In another hut, the corner of a large unoccupied bed with a Mickey Mouse counterpane could be seen.

'What's the matter, Rossman? Didn't I tell you that we're all New Naturists here?'

The general, naked, bawled at me as I entered the morning-room through the french windows. He stood at one end of the dining-table, emphasizing his words by poking his fork at a plate of steaming kedgeree. About ten men and twenty women, various ages, all of them naked, either smiled or frowned according to taste. I felt as if my black suit had caught fire. The maid, wearing only that frilly white thing that maids are supposed to wear in their hair, continued to deliver coffee in thin dark waterfalls.

'Rossman, if you're going to BG for me, you'd better hop out of those ludicrous togs in double-quick time. We believe in the skin here.'

I wanted to retreat, but I knew I had to stand my ground or something. I had to prove that I was worth my salary.

'I don't want to discuss this matter publicly, sir, if you don't mind. If you'll excuse me, sir, I'll go to my room and consider for a bit. I'm afraid I did not understand that nakedness was obligatory.'

It was really unforgivable of him to have announced my job, which depended on security, to a roomful of nudes. I crossed the room as quickly as possible, my body moving more awkwardly than usual, trying to avoid Annie's bloodshot eye, looking at nobody and so bumping accidentally, softly, into the maid. Just before I reached the door the general shouted:

'Consider? Obligatory? You're talking like a bloody butler, Rossman. You've been assigned to a job. Get stripped off, come down here and start guarding our bodies. And, for God's sake, Rossman, look cheerful about it.'

Half-defiantly I sat on my bed, considering. Certainly I had no obligation. I'd been cornered by sex again. I was shocked. Of course traditional values of modesty, such as applied in the fifties and sixties, and which I rather enjoy, had been eroded, but they had not, in those echelons where personal respect and privacy are valued, entirely disappeared. Far from it. Sure, nudes were commonplace enough at places like the seaside and universities. Discotheques had gone all-nude years before. There were even areas of London where nakedness was fashionable – Saturday morning in Ladbroke Grove, that kind of occasion. But all this nudity was on the unofficial, underground and often subvert side of the penny. You certainly didn't expect to find a nude in the Cabinet, and if you did you'd expect him to go naked on the quiet rather than declaring himself a New Naturist. For the New Naturists were extremists and, as such, under suspicion. They believed (like the Old Naturists) in going naked, but unlike the ON who look at each others' foreheads during conversations, they also believe in looking at other people's bodies and in the absolute maximum of physical contact. The essence of the New Naturist movement was inescapably orgiastic and therefore subversive. All of my training as a BG told me that I ought to contact Security and report this deviation. But surely Security knew that the Joint Minister of Education was swinging his skin all over the countryside? Well, I'd just have to collect evidence and report back as soon as possible. Meanwhile – was it going to be a New Naturist wedding, and if so, how could I guard the bride and groom? Revolvers woven into the hair of my armpits? Toe-nails sharpened and painted, by some cute and deadly manicurist, with arsenic? A blow-pipe protruding from my arse? I laughed to myself, but I was laughing at myself and that wasn't right. My aim, sometime in the ten years ahead, was to become the most respected bodyguard in the world, and already I was throwing away any chance of dignity. I began to imagine the ceremony in the little wood, rows of distinguished New Naturists, a few with medals, their shoulders touching as they whispered to each other:

'Who is that rather pointedly statuesque young man?'
'You mean the one attempting to lurk behind the gnarled oak?'
'That's the one.'
'Oh, that's Rossman, Lucy's special BG.'
'My goodness. Happy the bride . . .'

I grinned. I can laugh at myself. I determined that whether anyone laughed at me or not, I'd tackle any job with Whitehall stamped on it. For a few minutes I'd been on the verge of turning prima donna. I'd have to keep that sort of behaviour until I'd earned a reputation. I stripped off and inspected myself in the mirror. My person is larger than average, circumcised and slightly redder than the rest of me, as if still smarting from the operation. I did not consider the rest of my body, of which I have never been ashamed. I walked up and down in front of the mirror, watching it. Walking slowly was acceptable enough. It was when I tried walking quickly and then running past the mirror that the joggling became flapping. Well, it was unlikely that I'd be called upon to run except in an emergency, and in an emergency everyone would be too busy dodging bullets and wishing they'd worn armour to bother about the movement of my parts. It wasn't my fault that my parts moved, they were movable parts when I got them. Nude, I descended the staircase, meeting the general halfway.

'I'm smiling, Rossman,' he said. 'Because I'm glad you saw

sense if not the light. No hard feelings, eh? Ha, ha! Let's shake hands. Remember, a New Naturist always establishes physical contact with fellow New Naturists. Touch up, touch up, and play the game, eh! 'Course, you're not a true New Naturist, but while you're here you'll find it best to mingle.'

'I understand perfectly, sir. I'm sorry to have appeared put out, but I was piqued that Security didn't brief me more adequately.'

'Let it go, Rossman. Follow me. You'd better come and meet your charges.'

I followed him up the stairs, keeping my distance, along a corridor hung with enormous, gold-framed photographs of nakedly disporting de Vere Cartwrights, down a spiral staircase, across the thigh-high grass of a lawn and through the doors of a crenellated gymnasium. Miss Lucy de Vere Cartwright, face half-veiled by gilded curls, was upside-down in the gym, swinging by her knees from a green trapeze. Her eyes, upside-down, looked like strange, uncut emeralds. Even upside-down, her breasts retained a reasonable shape, well, their shape upside-down wasn't at all like the shape they would be the right way up, but their geometry was still pleasing – rub my rhomboid, yes. Her swinging was assisted by tanned Annie and a rather shrivelled-looking Dent, who arrested the trapeze at her signal. She whirled on to the coconut matting with a lucid somersault and faced me as my brain, knocked somewhat sideways, was saying to itself: 'Sunset, Somerset, somersault.' She observed me for several days and nights, then smiled for an evening. She approached me, and as I saw she wanted to shake my hand, I moved it towards her. She took it gradually, with both her light palms. Her body was the colour of Blackpool sands, except for a slight bruise on her right shoulder, her lipsticked nipples, the tobacco patch of her pubic hair and the glaring green of her finger- and toe-nails. Since she was examining me so candidly, I examined her back, a necessary counter-offensive if I was to avoid blushing.

'Hello, Rossman. I'm Lucy. These are my six bridesmaids. Which do you like best?'

Keeping hold of my hand, she steered me round through 360 degrees, pointing them out and naming in turn each nude bridesmaid. At this point I had better catalogue the bridesmaids, otherwise you will become as confused as I was, and so will I. They were, in order of introduction:

1. Drusilla or Drucy as she was known to the other girls and the Joint Minister. Drusilla, the daughter of an Air Vice-Marshal, was heavy in the hips, breasts and buttocks. These fashionable rotundities were matched by the roundness and weight of her dark eyes and it was clear that most of the well-adjusted flesh in her legs and arms was muscular. She was slapping a punchbag as we were introduced, but she stopped, opened her wide mouth wider and returned to the quivering punchbag. Rather a businesslike girl, I judged, confident, useful in a tight corner.

2. Jonquil, the sister of the bridegroom and daughter of the Minister of Security. I'd seen her before, but always clothed. This made it more frightening to confront the glare of her body. A voice inside me said: You don't look on the naked daughter of the Minister of Security and live. But I did. Her legs were absurdly long and narrow, supple, culminating in a small belly. An elongated, slightly freakish waist, and arms which tapered away to nothing. Eyes circled with silver, full-bunched and miniature nose, all set in a pale and totally immobile face. Short black electric hair.

3. Vera, and there always has been something about that Christian name which, for me, reeks with grasping sex. This was the first Vera I'd seen who fitted my mental image. She lay on one of the gym mats, sweating and heaving frankly after some exertion, smiling darkly (how does a girl smile darkly, well with darkly lipsticked lips), the shadow of face fur on her upper lip, eyes which transmitted blackness, used thirty-year-old breasts with brown nipples, white shadows from a bikini drawing atten-

tion to her nudity, darkness between her thighs, the rambling bush, black painted toe-nails. She raised her torso to an angle of about 30 degrees with one hand and waved slowly with the other, so that her right breast lolled from side to side in a second greeting. She stared like an X-ray. Stretchmarks.

4. Bess, and by now I was concentrating hard, like a schoolboy studying missile recognition, to make sure I'd know which was which if I ever met them clothed. Bess's body was heavy and embarrassed. In the way she stood, in the way she extended her hand, there was an attempt at aloofness. Not one of your natural New Naturists. Her smile was forced and narrow between stout cheeks. She said: 'So nice...' turned away and plummeted over a vaulting-horse. Then she stood behind it, watching me. I think her bones were too big. She wasn't helped by a formal permanent wave. Bess had been employed by the general as personal BG to Jonquil during her visit.

5. Sue had slightly slanting eyes and the mouth of a troublemaker. She was tall and she moved lightly towards me, placed her long fingers on my shoulders and looked straight into my eyes. I'm not proud of my eyes, they are a vague colour and my eyelashes are stubby. They see bloody well, but they're not interesting to look at. I'd really rather she'd stared at my person. She was laughing silently as she hauled herself slowly closer to me until her nipples just brushed against the hairs of my chest. I looked down her body, a strange bird's eye view, good muscles there under the skin, not bulging, you understand, but muscles certainly, ready to be used in some good cause. I nodded and retreated. Suddenly, I felt the weight of a young female body on my back, legs clasping round my waist.

6. Maisie had dropped from the wall-bars and was encircling me from behind. I knew her name was Maisie, because as she landed on me, Lucy cried: 'There goes Maisie!' I couldn't see Maisie now, except for the slender arms locked over my chest and the grubby small feet in front of my belly, but I'd seen her out of the corner of my eye as she watched from the polished

yellow bars above, and I'd observed that she was smallbreasted, natural white-blonde, blue-eyed, agile and about sixteen. Her plunge, it seemed, was a signal. The rest of the girls and women, except Bess and Annie, dragged me to the ground. Lucy sat on my chest facing south. Maisie wriggled round to take custody of my right leg. Vera took my left leg. Jonquil and Drucy took an arm each. It would have been possible to shake them off before I fell to the ground or even while I was pinioned, but not without hurting one of them. Raising my head I could see the general on the trapeze, puffing a cigar. Annie and Dent had switched on a transistor and were dancing cheek to cheek. Bess was approaching slowly, grinning with only half her mouth. The rest of them, from their posts on my anatomy, stared inwards at my person like a group of mystics attempting levitation. I could feel that it was, against my will, growing. They made movements with their bodies so that it stretched itself until it was long and heavy on my belly, pointing to one o'clock if you count my navel as twelve. Bess took up an allfours position behind my head and began to swing her breasts heavily across my eyelids, bumping my nose, sliding over the surface of my lips. Not one of them attempted to touch my person. It lay there, pulsing desperately like an outwitted Houdini. Then Drucy, shifting slightly astride my right bicep, hummed a clear note. Other voices joined hers until a warm chord hung in the air. They began to chant, a wordless psalm like an undulating landscape, they moved with the chant and their movements moved my body until, untouched by anything but air, my helpless person spurted gleam across my belly. The chanting which surrounded me disintegrated into laughter and I laughed too, partly with an eccentric kind of happiness, because there was a purity about that untouched coming which pleased me. I saw a cereal packet marked Untouched by Human Hands, I saw an unmanned rocket soft-land on the curve of Venus and I remembered a story I'd heard about a Moroccan night-club star in the old days, who used to walk, naked except for a book, onto the stage and pretend to be reading the book while his person independently rose, began to throb and finally, amazingly, came of its own accord, which was the cue for him to close his book, bow and exit to envious applause – a notable mystic. Suddenly the girls released me and returned to their exercises, humming to themselves. I rolled onto my face on the rough matting, wiping myself surreptitiously. Perched on the green trapeze, the general clicked his stop-watch.

The incident, it turned out, was by way of initiation into an almost supernaturally orgiastic household. No more attempts on my manhood were made after that. I had qualified for the freedom of the estate and, like an invisible man, was able to wander unmolested and unquestioned from room to heaving room. During my explorations I collected documentary and photographic evidence of the Joint Minister of Education's energetic activities.

Three days before the wedding I was limbering up with the ladies in the gym when the general rushed in, calling my name:

'It's trouble,' he shouted. 'Come on, you wobbly women, there's a mob of villagers pouring over the west wall.'

The general was panting and red as we sprinted out through the gymnasium doors. To each of us he handed an Olympic javelin from a silver stack. We pounded up a mown slope, over a humpback bridge thrown across a stream, along a sandy track through a grove and into a wide stretch of high grass. Against the pink of the outer wall our invaders were outlined clearly, three bulky young men and one thin one, all dressed in muddy colours, hesitating between flight and attack. It seemed to me that I was running on huge feet across and through a damp cloud of green. White sun dominated the sky. My right fist tight around the plastic grip of my javelin, the nude bodies of my Amazon platoon speeding in my slipstream, we were a small, body-free army of half-flying creatures zooming towards four enemy lumps, useless thugs weighed down into their graves by their clothes. Without breaking the rhythm of my charge, I stamped my right sole on the ground and opened my throat into a yell of battle and the yell was instantaneously joined by soaring screams from the women and a muscular bellow, far behind, from the general. It was enough. The invaders nodded to each other and one of them walked two tentative paces forward, raising his right, empty hand in a gesture of peace learned from Western movies. I could not be sure that I was awake. The thin invader advanced a few more paces towards us and as his face approached it seemed more and more like the face of a Red Indian – the blackness of his eyebrows, the shape of his eyes, the changing shadows below his cheekbones. But his clothes were totally English, worn brown jeans and a blue shirt open at the neck. When he suddenly smiled, even his face became English. By now the general was alongside me, flesh steaming and javelin poised above his right shoulder.

'Surrender now, or we'll use the lot of you for dartboards,' he shouted.

The thin man moved his right hand towards his inside pocket. My javelin ripped open the back of his hand. His mouth squawled. They weren't professionals, otherwise we'd have been a heap of dead nudes. I clouted the thin man round the side of the jaw, sat on him, drew his pistol and aimed it at his confederates. They raised their beefy hands lugubriously. Then I felt a sharp pain in my thigh, knocked a hypodermic out of the thin man's hand, clouted him twice, dragged him to his feet and heaved him over my shoulder. It wasn't much of a victory, I had been trained for more spectacular battles, but my Amazons cheered. They couldn't see the mountainous future which lay ahead of me. I could.

As we marched them back to the house I said to the general:

'Shall I guard them, sir, while you phone the Yellows?'

His face puckered.

'We can deal with these bastards ourselves, Rossman. We've

never had to call the Yellows to the Castle and we never will. We look after ourselves, we defend ourselves, and I'll have none of those torture-happy, vomit-coloured goons in my play-park.'

One of the large invaders spoke up.

'General,' he said, 'I've got a letter which you might find interesting.'

His hands hovered lower. I dropped the thin man and stepped back.

I said: 'Hold it. Everyone stay where you are. Surround these characters, but keep your distance.'

They were good girls. They formed a circle, javelins inwards, round the four. My thigh was tingling and I guessed why. Suddenly one of the bigger men crumpled from the knees and lay still. That confirmed it. The invaders were stubbed on Oddwood, a recent combat drug. Oddwood worked like this, I think. I would emphasize 'I think'. In the first place it would usually be bought, on the underground market, as an oblong grey block. It would be chewed thoroughly, for several hours and then the massacred plug would be flushed or buried. It worked slowly. Tingling at first, pleasant shivering, then, numbness spreading, cruising down your arteries, fanning out along the lines of your nerves. You then entered the first period of Oddwood, during which you were free to do whatever you wanted to do, as usual, but more single-mindedly than usual. During this period your sensations were deadened – your nerves would respond to a high electric shock, but not to normal intensities of pain. Increasingly your mind would become dominated by one thought. That thought might be 'kill' or 'steal' or 'run' or 'eat' or whatever you felt obliged to concentrate upon. So for troops in action Oddwood might be a powerful aid. But unless morale was high 'run' might prevail over 'kill'. It was chancy. For lovers it was useless, the great switch-off – where can you travel to sexually when your nerves are out of action? (The only pay-off in this area I ever heard of was a man who combined a dose of Oddwood with some illegitimate grandson of benzedrine, which gave him a numb hard-on lasting six hours. This was interesting for his mistress, but, as he told me afterwards, boring for him.) Anyway, after the numb period comes a certain slow-down, which probably explained why these invaders hadn't acted more decisively. And then collapse, into a coma which could last twenty-four hours or beyond. During coma, dreams of an extraordinary brightness were often reported. The coma usually ended with a sense of pleasant awakening, and it was the dreams rather than the immunity to pain which motivated most of The Rot's Oddwood users. Sometimes, I recalled, Oddwood was taken as a jab. I rubbed my shivering thigh. By now I was probably entering the first stage of Oddwood. The implications were obvious. These invaders, if they were all on OW, were not the main threat, but an advance guard sent to put us out of action. I laughed, it was such a classically absurd attack. Granted that in about five, six or seven hours I'd be in a coma and if they OWed the rest of us, so would all the New Naturists. But that gave us plenty of time to call in reinforcements.

Back in the house, the general doled out arms, but every time I tried to tackle him about calling in the Yellows, he turned away from me and told me to shut up. I paid less and less attention to his obstinacy, until I was beating my fists together with bruising force and chanting: 'We must get the Yellows. We must get the Yellows.' The general slapped my face, but he couldn't stop me. Finally he stamped out of the room, so I simply picked up the phone and called the local Yellow base. Then I went over to the window and called: 'Come on, come on.' About three-quarters of an hour later four Yellow prowlers swarmed up the drive. I allowed myself to collapse onto the carpet. It must have been a big jab.

My head was plagued with dreams. Vast insects made of human flesh clambered over each other in trembling hillocks. Commander Gray, his legs each a mile long, stood astride a motorway jammed with armoured-cars. Amber-coloured lightning struck through my skull and out through the soles of my feet. Two different sections of my brain seemed to be engaged in a mortal argument about whether or not to pick up something from the floor. The object they were arguing about kept changing, sometimes it would be an ashtray, sometimes a glass paperweight, sometimes the corpse of a girl, Lucy, Annie, Bess, Sue, Vera, Annie, Maisie, Drucy, Annie, Jonquil, Jonquil, Jonquil, Jonquil.

When I woke up my body was covered by a blanket. I saw a man who looked just like Finn, but he wore the uniform and goggles of a Yellow ranker.

'You must try wearing clothes sometime,' he said. Then he turned and marched out of the room. I think I passed out again. Anyway, the next thing I remember is the general, seated at his desk, fully dressed, his head slumped in his hands. Beside the desk stood a young man with very thin hair, his suit immaculate, his face explosive with red spots. When he moved, he moved badly, like a man with a limp which is more habit than hurt, or that results more from deformity than pain. His mouth was slightly open and some of his teeth were missing. There was a sense of venom about him. But that suit was perfect, it had been cut with care, so that it was hard to imagine the marred jumble of lines which his body probably made beneath it. This suit presented a smooth, midnight surface which was only broken on the left lapel by the letter M, shining turquoise bordered by silver. It was a badge I'd seldom seen before, but I knew what it meant. Media Police. All that power in skinny, blotched hands.

At Yellow Headquarters I wasn't questioned for long. Apparently the general had been plotting a peculiarly demented little coup. He had invested his wealth in an erotic photo magazine and taken over as editor. The twist was simply that he had obtained compromising photos of most of the members of the government who were trying to brand the New Naturists as illegally subvert, and was about to publish the pictures in *Skin*, his newly acquired magazine.

'What'll happen to him?' I asked the Media Policeman.

'He'll be off to the Hebrides. He can be as naked as he likes up there. Naked as a fish on a hook.'

'And the girls?'

'That depends. Most of them didn't know what was going on. The ones that did, well we'll find something for them.'

I wasn't sure what he meant by that.

I said: 'Will there be some kind of trial?'

He laughed and said: 'You won't be needed if there is. We're throwing you right back to the Ministry of Education. They need all the BGs they can lay their chalky hands on.'

Now I was back in my clothes, I didn't feel bothered by the bloke. For one thing, I was twice as big.

'Look, did I do anything I shouldn't have done? I was assigned and I played it as straight as I could.'

Skinny twisted the corners of his mouth.

'What was your assignment?'

'To guard the general and his household.'

'Nothing else?'

'Guard his property.'

'And you a top graduate from Hollow Hill? What about guarding the State? This time I'm giving you the benefit of the doubt, but as soon as you found that the general was running a bollock farm, you should have reported back to the chainwork. Anyone you're set to guard is important enough for you to investigate.'

'I checked on phone calls, letters, visitors and all that. I've handed in my file, haven't I? I couldn't have carried it much farther, or I'd have been caught with my hand in his desk or his daughter and kicked over the wall—'

'—We'd have looked after you if—'

'It's more complex than you think. I don't like what I did much. It was a basic slash at the BG-target relationship. You're not a BG, you don't know. But a BG has to be obsessive, he has to think all the time, worry constantly about his target, where's that target, is he drinking too much, is he sick and if he's sick which hospital has the security he needs? You have to nag your own head about him like a mother with a baby, you have to get like some timid wife whose husband's three hours late and hasn't phoned. Now if you're going to push yourself into that state about your target, and you'd better, because if you don't you're going to go loose and then you might as well forget it, if you're going into that state about your target, you've got to build up some respect for him, no messing. And it has to be real respect. All right, I'm giving you a lecture but you need one before you start telling any more BGs how they ought to act. And about that real respect. It's quite likely that your target may not have many of the qualities you admire, he may treat you like a turd, take no notice, your efficiency depends on unbreakable invisible links with that man. You have to find something about him you can respect, and grip on to that.'

'Like Annie Beauvais' tit?'

'She offered it to me. Were Annie and Dent in on this thing with the general?'

'I interviewed them together. High-speed interview too. They stood up very well, kept their story going. They said they'd take one of my men to the general's secret radio transmitter. They drove him to the woods, smashed his head in and then did a vanishing act. They're the ones we want. They were using the general. He wasn't much more than a dirty old man and a drunk.'

I was about to shout at him, but I swallowed it back.

'It's OK,' he said, 'you can break those unbreakable invisible links now. You're not working for Patch any more.'

'What's happened to Jonquil?'

He raised a sparse eyebrow.

I said: 'You know, the daughter of the Minister of Security.'

He said: 'I'm not receiving you. I didn't hear that. But don't say it again.'

Back at the Ministry I found myself in a waiting-room with Finn Murdoch, now in civilian clothes with too many colours dyed and woven into them.

'They thought I'd gone over the top,' he said, talking fast and low and grinning in flashes. 'Somebody told them I took my holiday too seriously. They had some down on Annie too, poor little fish, chucked her out of the bowl, splash, gasp, but she got some job as a secretary. They pulled me off BG duty and shoved me in the Yellows for a stint of skull-bashing. But they knew they'd have to take me back, I'm too good, honest. My record's watertight bordering on sensational. One time I brought down two assassins in three seconds and they were working from opposite sides of the hall. It's in the files. Well, some of them don't like that sort of reflex action of course, they say I'm too damn quick, they think I fire on suspicion, all right you have to fire on suspicion now and then, otherwise I suspect you're for the slab.'

We were called in to see Masters, the general's replacement. I wasn't encouraged by the interview. For one thing I knew that working with Finn would strain me, he was friendly enough but he'd been in the game long enough to make me play dummy. For another thing, the new Joint Minister was such a grey blob of a man – very hard for a BG if he can't be sure at any given moment whether his target is dead or alive. Another thing, I didn't know whether Finn knew about my holiday report on him and Annie. Another thing, the Ministry of Education hadn't brought me much luck so far. Another thing, education bores me.

In the split second before Masters let me grasp his hand I could feel the coldness radiating from his skin. His office carpet was light-brown, a colour which nauseates me in a small way. Those eyes were dim and lacking in purpose, even his hair seemed half-hearted. There was no cloud of action above this man. He was, considering his position, extremely unknown. Only the most heavy-headed newspapers had written articles about him, only one of which I had managed to read. In his career he had kept a straight bat and scored singles only. His hobby was watching cricket. He read books about education and had written one. Reduced to panic in the face of overwhelming dullness, the writer of the article had concentrated on how much his wife had helped him and the personalities of his four vividly contrasting cats.

I sat straight as Masters told us his plans, noticing that Finn had shifted his arse to the front of his chair, stretched out his legs and was crossing and uncrossing his ankles with some interest. The route of the Joint Minister's imminent tour through educational establishments did not sound dangerous. One teachers' training college, women only, small and A Class, one C-Stream Primary, and a very new university which, he hastened to assure us, was the best-behaved college in the country, with a super-tight security system of its own. At each stop the Joint Minister would make a speech composed by the Ministry which would lay down, gingerly, some future policy lines. They would be factual and unemotional speeches. Their aim was not to hit out at subverts or gain publicity, but simply to put some plans on the record without fuss.

Whatever I felt, everything demanded that I should appear friendly to Finn. As we travelled north, Finn at the wheel of the Rolls, I told him:

'The North bothers me. Every time.'

'Know what you mean. You like the warm.'

'Not that exactly.'

'Those run-down, broken up cities rusting away, ruddy great iron buildings all black and stinking, windows broken, old bricks in every odd corner of the street, the kingdom of slumdom, the rotten heart of The Rot and all that?'

'It's really the people up there I don't fancy so much.'

'They're friendly.'

'That's right, they're friendly.'

'You walk into a London shop, they don't even look at you. They just keep swapping the shit with each other behind the counter. You go er hem, you cough, but you have to practically vomit before they turn on you looking as if they wish they had a gun in each fist and a licence to kill and shouting: "What you want then?" and in that word "then" there's a lot of hatred rolled up. But up North they look up when you come in and even smile sometimes, stranger or not, and pretty often they'll even stop counting money, lean over the counter and chat about whatever you like.'

'That's what I mean. When I go in a shop to buy something, box of matches say, I just want a box of matches and no nonsense. Not chat. If I want chat, if I want people, I can drop in the BG Club or wherever. If I want matches I go to a shop.'

'You're a frozen kind of cod, Thug.'

'No. I like to do one thing at a time. If I'm buying matches I like to say: "Matches, please," put down my money and walk out with matches. Be even quicker getting them from a vendomat of course.'

'Cold as the black half of the moon.'

'Listen, Finn, if you owned a shop you'd spend your time on monologues for the customers. Not me. I'd give them the quickest service in the postal district, streamlined and straight. No chat, no messing. Keep the business moving like a monorail. Unless of course I wanted a particular item of information from one of my customers. Then I'd chat all right, but it would be deliberately aimed chat. But say I've got a shop, you're a customer, that's not basically a friendly relationship. Friends ask for credit, friends take up your time when you should be planning for expansion. You own the shop so you want to watch that the customers don't steal the counter, you want to watch they don't spit on the floor, you want to watch they're not watching to see if you've got a double lock on the door or where you hide your overnight takings. And they should be watching you back, seeing you give them the right weight and the right change.'

Finn looked out of the window. Then he said:

'I think that everything everyone does is political.'

I didn't feel that called for an answer. We pulled in to a motorway service station. Finn stayed in the car while Masters took me into the VIP section, separate entrance, right by the Yellow Block. As we drank our coffee, Masters gave me a look which could mean he didn't like me or could mean simply nerves. My size makes a certain type of person nervous. I gave a polite smile in return; I wasn't bothered. It was a job. Then he said:

'I'm sorry that I find it hard to make conversation. I would enjoy talking to you, but I am immensely shy.'

He blushed and shut up. I was touched and glad. Now I had a couple of sentences to cling on to which made me like my target. I couldn't admire him wholeheartedly, but at least I could like him for the small courage which enabled him to say those words. They had obviously been rehearsed under his breath over and over, and perhaps he had used them before. I said:

'Doesn't matter, sir, I'm not a great one for talk.'

But he seemed to want conversation. I made another effort, thinking first if we had anything in common. Education was the obvious key word, but that meant going back a bit.

'What was your best subject at school, sir?'

'Er . . . Greek. Ancient Greek, you know.'

'Oh yes, I know. That must be very . . . all about gods and heroes and so on, I suppose. I didn't take any Greek.'

'No . . . but more and more of the youngsters are taking it now. It's not very useful to them in itself, I suppose, but very beautiful. Like another planet.'

'I'm afraid I'll have to settle for this world, sir.'

He didn't laugh. 'Of course their degrees are very useful.'

'I believe a lot of Greek scholars find their way into Security, sir.'

'A good classics degree, as the chairman of ICI said only last year, is a guarantee of intellectual quality. A platitude, of course. I specialized early. I loved it.'

'Sir.'

'Sometimes Greece seems more real to me than England. Ancient Greece I mean of course, not Red Greece.'

I'm no archaeologist, but I wanted to dig into Masters. So I said:

'What was Ancient Greece like, sir?'

Then he smiled. 'There weren't many people at all. It was a slow, agreeable society. It had a kind of certainty. I think the Greeks were very open people. I imagine them walking through calm, stone streets under a dome of sunlight.'

He stirred his coffee, produced a tube from his pocket and shook himself a happy pill. I noted the brand-name, Millpond.

'Excuse me sir, but it's important for me to know your details if I'm going to work well. Do you use any other pills?'

'Millpond once or twice a day, depending on the pace. A Snip before meals to cut appetite. And a couple of Oceans before I go to bed.'

'Where d'you buy them?'

'I send my secretary, usually. Sometimes buy them myself.'

'I'll buy them in future, sir, if it's all right with you. Much too easy to slip you a Micky. I'll bulk-buy directly from the Health Ministry. I've got a contact.'

He sighed, nodded, stood up and led the way back to the car. He'd been enjoying his tiny excursion to Ancient Greece, I suppose.

Our first stop was the teachers' training college. One glance through that hall of eighty girls and you could bet that they were more interested in Finn, propped against a pillar, like a grinning lighthouse, whistling inaudible melodies to himself, than they were in revolution. I should say that about ten per cent of them were either eyeing Finn or whispering about him while Masters, head down, ploughed through his brief, informative speech. His theme was competition in education and life. He thought that although competition had been a dirty word in intellectual circles during the 'sixties and early 'seventies, successful competition was necessary for the evolution of a guiding class.

The what class? Don't you mean a ruling class?

No, he didn't say that. He said 'a guiding class'. He said the government was in favour of many different kinds of school, both privately-owned and state-run. 'There are a thousand different kinds of child,' he said, 'therefore we need a thousand different kinds of school.' He looked up when he said that, so we applauded. He then went on to outline the new selection system, under which children would take one major examination every year to discover whether they were still suited to their class, their stream and their school. Afterwards we took sherry with the Principal. She was about forty and rather beautiful in a well-used way. After saying how much he liked the sherry and the college grounds, Masters said:

'How do you react to the Ministry's examination proposals?'

She turned away from him, refilled her tulip-shaped sherry glass, knocked it back and said:

'Sweet Jesus fucking Christ. I'm getting drunk tonight, but I'll write you my resignation in the morning.'

Masters looked at me and Finn.

'I'm perfectly willing to forget you said that.'

She outstared him.

'Don't you ever bloody forget it.'

We left quickly. Masters was trembling. Finn, although he smiled at the occasional trainee teacher in the corridor, seemed more serious than usual. I said as lightly as I could:

'Hysterical spinster. That's what the change of life does for you.'

Neither of them said anything.

The C-stream primary school was smack in the middle of

Manchester. Trouble seemed possible. Manchester has a subvert reputation despite its crack Yellows. This school, with three thousand kids, was scarred by petrol bombs from last year's rioting. The Yellows on the gate waved us through and the headmaster, a big man with a stubble haircut and tweeds, greeted us with a fierce handshake. In his study he produced a crumpled piece of exercise-book paper and passed it to Masters. It was a scribbled death threat to the Joint Minister.

'Haven't traced him yet,' said the headmaster. 'The note only came yesterday. Pushed under that door. What do you want done about it, security-wise?'

Masters looked uncertain.

I said 'Excuse me, can we check the programme?'

The headmaster said: 'First the Minister's speech to the kids. Then presentation of prizes. Then a tour of the school.'

I said: 'We can cut the tour.'

Masters said: 'Oh, but I think—'

I said: 'Sir, there are three thousand of those kids. If they're planning to bump you they'll wait till you're on the tour. Much easier. I'd ask for one more special precaution. That five minutes before you arrive on the platform, the headmaster orders that all kids at the back of the hall move to the front and vice versa.'

Finn said: 'Makes sense to me.'

It was agreed. This time the Joint Minister's speech was even shorter. For the benefit of the kids he talked about patriotism and its opposite. For the record he talked about the setting up of junior cadet forces in primary schools. He did not mention examinations. Then, still standing behind his reading desk, Finn seated on one side of him and myself on the other, he began to present prizes. As he was handing *The Encyclopaedia of Rocketry* to a largish ten-year-old engineering scholar, the boy whipped a bread-knife from the inside of his blazer and began to rip it through the air towards the Joint Minister's throat. I got to him before Finn, grabbed the boy's arm before his knife hit flesh, twisted that arm up behind him with all my strength, lifted him off his feet and hurled him off the platform, where Finn sat on him. It could happen anywhere, any time. That wasn't the end. When the boy came out of hospital, he was, of course, stashed straight into a Rehabilitation Camp. But his photo, blown up from one of those school-group jobs, began to appear in schools all over the country, pasted up in lavatories, stuck on noticeboards, pinned to the underside of desks. His face entered Rot legend. You couldn't blame the headmaster for failing to spot the little killer. It wasn't even as if the lad's parents were detainees. His father was a double-checked stockbroker and his mother, well his mother was nothing much, she'd never done anything since she left school apart from having a couple of children. Security watched her for two years after the attempted bump, but she still did nothing. She seemed sad, obviously. How would you like to spend all your love on a ten-year-old monster?

That night Masters took to his bed early. Finn and I drank slow whiskies in the hotel bar.

'That was good sudden work today, Thug,' he said. 'I'll say that for you, you're certainly sudden. Should get a bonus for that.'

'I don't care. Get a living wage, don't I?'

'But you'll be wanting a house sometime. You know, one of those old brick ones with a wife to match and a couple of kids for private schools and two cars for the garage. And then you'll want to insure all that. And raise gun dogs or something. That's what you're meant to want.'

'No. It's funny. I don't want that at all. It – it's not that it scares me or anything like that, it just doesn't interest me. It's just blank to me.'

'Don't you want to get married?'

'I like a woman now and then, but not all the time, Finn. I don't want anything in my way. Don't want anything holding me back or on my back.'

'Holding you back from what? Where do you want to go?'

'Look, I'm not used to defending myself. Just because I don't want to collect property, that doesn't make me a Red. Property's all right, but I can do without it. And just because I don't want marriage, that doesn't make me an unconscious homosexual or anything.'

'Oh Thug, you're such a gruesome disappointment to me. I always thought you were the biggest Commie queer in the business.'

'I can take sex, but you can't leave it alone.'

'I *know* you can take sex. I *know* you're not a perve. After all, you made it with Annie Beauvais, didn't you?'

I ignored that one. I didn't think it was good for our friendship if he made fun of me like that. And I didn't want to talk about Annie. So I said:

'Finn, I'll tell you exactly what I want. I want to be the best bloody bodyguard in this country.'

He squinted at me through his whisky.

'That shouldn't be hard. But what's the next step after that?'

'Nothing else. I just want to be the best.'

'And known as the best, I suppose.'

'Well, acknowledged as the best. In the business. And I want the best BG job that's going and that's all I want.'

'Don't you see that you're limiting yourself? You're playing safe. There's too little competition. Most BGs are deadheads.'

'I am limited. I don't mind that. I like the territory within my limits. Anyway, what about you?'

'Yeah, I'm limited too, but I don't care about that. I want to move into politics, take history by the scruff of the neck and shake it till it yells. I want to buy an island and build boats. I want to marry four women, three big and one little and I want to open an antiquarian bookshop on Mars and I want to drink a bar dry and wake up in the morning to find myself a member of the Royal Family and I want to have my own show on television, an hour every night at midnight just doing exactly what I want to do.'

'Anything else?'

Finn looked wickedly around him, at the moustached barman, the rich old people with their coffee and liqueurs, the military contingent of sharp officers and the man with a head like a cardboard box who might have been a salesman or an actor. Then he raised his glass and shouted at the top of his voice:

'I'll tell you what I want, Rossman. I want you to be my own personal bodyguard.'

The approach to the University of the Lakes sticks hard in my head. We drove evenly up a pass. As we rose, the pass narrowed. We came into the shadow of the shoulders of the mountains. A waterfall was crashing heavily above us, ducking under the road through a stone tunnel, then bombing down to a breakneck river. Bulging, irregular walls of dark rock slabs lined the road. The vast black cloud above the car ended abruptly as we hit the summit of the pass and saw, opening before and below us, the green-based oval valley, its mild lake specked with sails. Around the far end of the water clustered the bright blocks, bridges and towers of the university, white, silver and summer-blue. Graceful jetties. A dome of fragmented, every-coloured glass. Canopied walkways curving through the air. On three sides, mountains. That remains one of the best moments in my life. It was a pure vision of the future England which I loved even more than the England of the present, for which I was ready to die and prepared to kill. Looking around the car, I noticed that the others were smiling too. Masters and I both found ourselves reading the sign aloud: 'The University of the Lakes', as we reached the swing-gates and our passes were checked by a young, loose-limbed Yellow with the distorted grin of a gum-chewer.

Quietness. There was a quietness in the way these students talked and moved, as if the mountains were listening and so words and gestures must be chosen as carefully as a jeweller chooses sapphires. And you noticed a glow about them, in them, on them. Their clothes were different from the severe fashions of the cities, cream-coloured soft clothes with occasional bands of violent colour, loose-fitting, almost robes, extremely clean, not uniforms because they were all cut differently, and yet uniforms all the same because of the universal colour of cream. Pink faces, either much exposed to the valley winds or flushed with central heating. They hardly looked at us, and yet doors were always opened for us by some distant-looking student, girl or boy. The Vice-Chancellor welcomed us into his office of glass furniture and white paint. It was ghostly and it was beautiful.

This time it was champagne rather than sherry. Masters shifted his glass from hand to hand, sipped and said:

'Oddly, it makes me feel nervous.' The Vice-Chancellor laughed formally.

'Not odd at all. An unexpected place. Very few visitors. Very little publicity. We deliberately keep the emotional temperature turned down low.'

'Yes, it's placid.'

'Exactly. An excellent atmosphere for constructive thought. And naturally anyone from the troubled world outside finds the peace of the place a little unnerving at first.'

'However, I can already appreciate its beauty.'

'Yes, it has beauty. Charm? Probably not. Charm implies a certain frivolity which we lack. But grace, certainly. Beauty, undoubtedly. And the world outside, from here, seems jagged, unsafe, ugly and violent. Very few of our students are happy to leave, even for vacations. And that's about all I can tell you, of course.'

Of course. The government would hardly create such a magnificent machine for the sake of turning out lawyers or musicians. The isolation of the place, its reputation for taciturnity and the feeling you received of being in a space-station all meant that the university must be an important weapon in the external or internal security chainwork. The Joint Minister had only come so that he could make a speech and present degrees. If it was thought that he knew the secrets of the place, his life would be twice as risky. On the way to our quarters, we passed a group of green-painted metal domes. Masters looked straight ahead as we passed them. Finn and I were bound to observe more. Even in this place we had to watch out for the odd lunatic sniper.

Next day Masters chatted laboriously about the need for more specialized universities, including military academies of the modern kind and he touched upon the closure of some of the unnecessary universities. Then a line of men and women in cream robes took scrolls from Masters. The students were as poised as saints. They made Masters look like a shaking stinging-nettle in a field of orchids. There was a strength about them, it seemed to be centred in their eyes. I recognized it as willpower, or was it concentration, or was it certainty? Whatever it was, they all seemed to have taken it and made it a part of themselves.

Just as we left, strolling across the mosaic paving of a quadrangle, I glimpsed Commander Gray. There was no mistaking the manner in which the hair on the back of his neck jutted over the collar of his dark-red uniform. He didn't see me, and, although I shouted a greeting, he didn't turn round.

Back in the car, Finn lit a cigarette and said:

'That's one hell of a spooky joint. If I was sent to search for the Holy Ghost, that's where I'd start.'

Masters was subdued, as if he'd been stunned by strangeness. Three days after we returned to London I was called to Security.

Security said: 'You're looking good. We're putting you on permanent Stateroll. And we've got a new target for you. Lots of loot and fun facilities.'

'I've only been with Masters for a week. I'm settling. And it's not fun I'm after.'

'We've decided to transfer you.'

'Why?'

I knew it was none of my business, but I wanted to know.

'This new gig needs everything you've got. You'll find a lot of holes. Sew them up.'

'I want to stay with Masters.'

Security shrugged.

'Don't let's waste Stateroll's time. You know I don't argue. Come back tomorrow with your mind wide open.'

I went straight over to Education, flashed my pass at a few faces and walked into Masters' office. Finn was in an armchair, a comic book in his left hand and, because I hadn't knocked, an automatic in his right. Masters stood up.

I said: 'I think some computer at Security is having a trauma. Over there they're saying they don't want me to be your BG.'

Masters said: 'We have to do what Security thinks is right.'

I looked right through him, turned and marched the hell out of Education. Heard footsteps behind me, looked and saw Finn.

'Tough luck, but they'll find you something with a bit more propulsion.'

'Why the hell am I being shuttled around like this? I'm guaranteed straight. I've got qualifications.'

Finn said: 'It's just a personality thing, Thug.'

'What do you mean?'

'You scare Masters out of his fur-lined pants. Simple as that. He doesn't mind me, he even chats to me. But he's been having nightmares, real Gormenghasts. And in those nightmares, you're the star.'

'What did I do?'

'You know, you did your duty. At the school. That kid with the knife. He dreams about that. When you picked him up and slammed him down on the floor. There was a kind of breaking noise if you noticed it. Masters dreams that you keep heaving that kid into the air and banging him down, over and over. Only the way Masters dreams it, Masters is the kid with the knife.'

I said: 'Thanks,' Finn said: 'Good luck,' and I went back to work it out with Security. Suddenly I was glad to be shot of Masters. I saw him now as an over-age schoolboy (without a knife) and the small respect I'd accumulated for him evaporated. It may be a sign of my immaturity that I've always searched for a target to whom I could devote my life, but I'm trying to be honest. In a way it is a wish for security, a dissatisfaction both with myself and my targets. The ideal situation for a BG seems to me that of the so-called gorillas who used to guard General De Gaulle. They were serving a great man and they knew it, they had stuck by him through his exile and his triumphs and they had a real job to do – that is, they were there to fight a genuine, constant danger and not to do battle with the shadows thrown by their target's neuroses.

That night, with the briefing on my new target slammed tight in the tin drawer at the back of my head, I went down to the Whitehall BG Club. I was between jobs, I could let go, turn off my engines and wallow a bit.

I stood alone at the bar and broke habit by studying not one of the other faces. Watching myself in the mirror, I stood with my feet apart, evenly balanced. The mirror returned my smile. Balance is a word I like, I've written it on my bedroom wallpaper, in a fat purple-crayon scrawl, BALANCE. Contemplating that word I saw pictures, moving pictures of myself at my best. Sometimes spectacular balance – the time I stood in my yellow armour on the sixteenth-storey hotel ledge staring upwards, waiting for eleven minutes until the Trot sniper on the roof edged too far forwards and my two bullets unlocked the top of his skull. That took balance in the mind as well, waiting, eyes fixed to the end of his rifle barrel, waiting, as his left elbow, forearm and hand became visible in silhouette, resisting the temptation to wound, and waiting, inevitably, until he had to look down to see what was happening immediately below him, and then, the instant his dark hair showed above the horizon of the roof edge, swinging my body backwards as far as possible, toes on the ledge and left hand clamped on the window-frame, leaning back to get a point-blank reward for all that waiting and then swinging myself in and through the window as bits of brain and bone dropped to the street. And sometimes, much more often, the kind of satisfying but unspectacular balance which means nothing to the onlooker unless he tries trouble. I mean the bodyguard's technique, very like a soccer goalkeeper's, of holding his body ready to leap or dive in any direction. A bodyguard's poise, with all his senses open. A bodyguard's awareness of the balance of a situation, the balance of a room's calm, the balance of his own body – that's the test, that often saves him from fatal boredom, just the consciousness that at every step he takes his body must be ready, an almost unattainable ideal, but ideals would be pretty bloody dull if you ever did attain them. And inside the balance of the bodyguard stands, like a steel spring, his will to action. I am not afraid of anything, but that's not so exceptional, and the fearful man can usually wipe out most of his fear, if only temporarily, with drugs. I think I have a rarer quality. I cannot be bored.

You'd better rest now.

I'd rather not. I want to keep going now.

You must be tired. You mustn't try too hard.

I'd rather carry on. Unless, I mean, is there an instruction that I should stop? Can't I go on?

Of course you can go on. But we want you to get well again.

Will I be able to take these bandages off my eyes soon?

We'll take them off as soon as it's safe.

Thank you. Yes, I'll go on now.

You were in the bar at the BG Club.

Yes. Around me I could hear the latest BG gossip, the latest BG jokes. Most of the talk centred on the General Election, since many of these BGs had been assigned to Members. I had no interest in the election as such – it was a pleasant ritual which would confirm the All-Party Government's majority – but its security aspects were intriguing. The growth of the bumping wave meant that public meetings could be entered by ticket only, and normally only about a hundred tickets would be issued, all to trusties. A big meeting would be watched by the general public on closed circuit, the candidate usually speaking from a small back room, although he might not even be in the building or the city, you couldn't tell, he might only be present on videotape. Mutual trust between speaker and audience is hard to establish in such conditions. It's also tough titty on the candidate who can't afford the requisite electronics. He just has to take his chances. But I have an intuition that people will flock to a meeting when there is some chance of disturbance, even assassination. The tight-rope walker without a safety net. We all share a taste for death. And most of the major political figures at that time forced themselves to walk the rope occasionally. These were the big men, striving to build their images to prime-minister size or bigger. They exploited that sense of danger, sometimes flamboyantly, stepping out from behind a bullet-proof rostrum to deliver a particularly passionate passage or actually walking through the body of the hall at the end of a popular speech, shaking hands with people on the aisles. Naturally the aisles would be lined with BGs and my own belief is that many of the papers bearing death threats which orators waved so defiantly were written by their own speech-writers. But melodrama often works. The one ancient tradition which had completely disappeared from elections was baby-kissing. A young mother had wheeled her pram into the path of the safe New Tory MP for a Surrey constituency, the Junior Minister of Health in fact. He had kissed the baby for luck and votes, and even gone so far as to lift it out of its pram and dandle it in front of the cameras. It was lucky that photographs were taken. Shortly after the incident the Junior Minister became violently ill. The mother, identified from the photos, was arrested and admitted, under Yellow cross-examination, that her baby had been infected by the outbreak of pneumonic plague from her neighbourhood Microbiological Research Station.

On my left-hand side, two lumpish BGs on barstools were

exchanging BG jokes. Most of such jokes are blackish, that is, they work by offering a negation of BG concepts of duty towards one's target or by ridiculing security. I don't like these jokes, not that I do not have a sense of humour, but because I want, above all, to preserve my seriousness about my vocation. Jokes should be kept in their place. This is a typical BG joke:

OLDHAND BG
I see your target got bumped, son. Who goofed?

YOUNGHAND BG
We thought everything was granulated (trans: taken care of). He was in querencia (trans: the safest place of all). We built him a suit of customized brickwork, wound him around with 1,000 metres of electric barbs, set him on wheels and were pushing him along Security Tunnel Z 17 when suddenly – (Younghand BG breaks into dry sobs)

OLDHAND BG
So who goofed?

YOUNGHAND BG
You're not going to eat this. But suddenly, round the corner, its neck lowered to the horizontal, newly-detonated grenades clipped on to its horn-things, galloped a giraffe which had been braved up on LSD. It reached right over the wirework, licked the target and exploded.

OLDHAND BG
An acidhead giraffe with headmines? But that's the oldest trick in the book!

I have to admit it, I like to hear the old jargon, even though the stories don't please me because of my attitude. The whisky, however, was making me more tolerant. Like the reporter, the

BG spends so many hours with his colleagues that naturally he develops a private language. I looked around me for the first time that evening, with some warmth, at my fellow-BGs. We are a special race. Among people who attend meetings and debates to listen to words, we watch eyes and hands and the movements of eyes and hands. Among all the people who are walking from A to B along a street, we alone do not care whether we are at A or B or in between, we have no destination, we are always *there,* alongside our target. If you were a BG I wouldn't have to explain this, you'd know. I don't believe that astronauts ever feel they have to express their mutual trust in words. Words can't reach the depths of such trust.

There was a sudden displacement of weight by the crowd beside the door and in came two strangers, one bald and waddling, Egyptian camera round his neck, the other lean and wearing a nicotine-impregnated moustache. They whispered to the barman, then bought three drinks, including a big whisky for me. They represented the *Daily Mirror*. I told the photographer to hang fire for the moment.

The lean reporter said: 'Education pushed us a commercial for that bumping bid by that schoolkid. We've got their OK to depth you for a hero-piece if that's all right with you.'

He unfolded a letter with the official heading. It had been signed on behalf of Masters. Now, it's as well to stay on remote but nodding terms with photographers and reporters. Learn their faces by heart, the same ones, *Times* or *Mirror*, will bob up again and again. I've noticed that their faces age quickly, but they remain puffily agile compared with office workers, their energy coming from their nerves, while the BG's energy springs from his general fitness. It's common for a BG to have to elbow a photographer, or even snatch his camera and expose the film, but photographers are understanding little blokes. Camera breaking is almost always unnecessary. If a BG avoids bad blood with the press, there are advantages. He can always double-check a new photographer's credentials by referring to other photographers. (Cameras are ideal explosives containers.) He should talk to reporters, but normally only in the shallowest way, on the level of some improvement in the weather being possible or where to get a meal or a lay after nine o'clock in the same provincial deadwater. Now and then I pass on racing tips to the press and vice versa. By now they know that I'm not likely to give them anything deeper than that. The older pressmen call me, ironically considering my physical bulk, Jockey. I doubt if more than three or four of them know my right name. If I'm asked my name by some young reporter I say The Hulk or Mary Queen of Scots or something, always a different and comical name, and the other reporters laugh, as a rule. Most reporters have a sense of humour. Most photographers do too, but they carry it too far. Anyway – if a BG is wounded on duty, the friendship of the press may be a help in getting a doctor quickly. But if a BG is so carried away by his role in public life that he feels he must exude massive menace all the time, he is not only acting unprofessionally by proclaiming his function brashly, underlining the possible dangers of a situation and thus encouraging them by putting the idea of danger into the heads of the public, he is also building a bad gangster-image for his target and alienating the press, who don't mind man-mountains so long as they show that they're marginally human and unlikely to maim the gents of the press. Chattiness, however, should be avoided.

I agreed to an interview, provided they cleared it with Education after it was written, but I stuck fast for no photo. Obvious reasons. So the photographer scaled a barstool, ordered another round and watched. The reporter began:

'Now, we've got the straight facts of the thing from Masters' office. It's not the first time they've tried to bump him and it won't be the last, but it's the first time they've used a kid. Now, you've been around, you know the lay-bys and sideways of The Rot, who do you think is behind this one?'

'I didn't talk to the kid, I just—' I gave a quick mime demonstration of what I did to the boy. 'I don't know who paid him. You'll have to ask the kid. I expect someone's asking him right now.'

'You think The Rot's getting stronger in the primary schools now?'

'It's getting strong everywhere where it isn't being cut down.'

'You believe the only answer is more security?'

There was a violent banging on the ceiling. I frowned up at it, then continued:

'I think we need to double both our defensive and offensive security. It seems to me—'

A piece of plaster shaped like the Isle of Wight smashed on the bar. A hole the size of a fist appeared in the ceiling, then it was football sized, then it was as big as an arm-chair. The men next to the door tried to get out. No good, the door had been furtively chained and padlocked from the outside. A three-foot diameter tube of flexible shining metal protruded through the hole in the ceiling. Everyone jammed into the corners of the bar. There was a roaring noise from above and suddenly the air of the bar was full of large and small yellow splotches, splashing over woodwork, suits and faces, whizzing lumps of cold, sticky, yellow mess. Using a barstool, I tried to grab at the end of the tube, but I was only rewarded by the sight of a head wearing a Mickey Mouse mask beside the tube and a sudden shower of concentrated gunk. Two BGs began systematically battering-ramming their bodies against the door. By the time it had been broken and we made our yellow-blotched way up the stairs to the room above, the character in the Mickey Mouse mask had vanished. In the centre of the room, still roaring and pumping out its sickening load down into the bar, stood a kind of four-wheeled, shining, giant vacuum cleaner, its control lever shaking at a line marked BIG BLOW. The photographer, by now, was berserk with delight.

'Gentlemen,' I said. 'This looks like the work of – John Custard.'

Afterwards we were all too busy washing custard out of our hair and brushing it off our suits to take any anti-publicity steps. Next day the *Mirror* carried a centre-page colour spread of custard-covered BG pics. I was very quietly very angry. The Press could be relied upon to honour D-notices, and put down most brands of subversion – but when a Rot upsetter like John Custard comes along, they all fall for his gimmick. He's even becoming something of a folk-hero. One of the big comic-book houses even started featuring a similar knockabout subvert among their super-heroes. Security soon put a stop to that. That bloke bothers me, well not seriously, he can't do much harm so long as he sticks to custard, it's just that I can't understand such in-depth tomfoolery, you know, he's risking rehabilitation every time he flings a kersplosh at a politician or a BG or whoever. And it's all planned down to the punctuation, he gets away with it. He could be killing, you realize that, don't you? But he sticks to slapstick. I'd like to catch him.

What would you do with John Custard if you caught him?

I'd, I'd get him all tied up first. That would be the first thing. You know my head's hurting again. Can I have that next injection?

I'll ring for the nurse.

She wears perfume, you know. I didn't think they were allowed to wear perfume, nurses.

Don't you like perfume?

It's not that. It doesn't worry me. It just seems out of place. I think of hospitals as being very clean and white and bare. Is this hospital like that?

More or less. But you've got a room of your own. You're a special patient.

And the nurse is allowed to wear perfume? I don't mind. It's just that it's not what you expect. In a bedroom, yes, you expect it, perfume I mean.

I'll ask her not to wear perfume if you like.

What does she look like? Is she one of those lumping great matron-types? She never says anything much.

She's quite pretty. I'll ask her to stop wearing perfume. Here she comes.

John Custard, yes, that's where we got to last time. And my new job, that's what I was coming to. Well, after that custard machine I was bad-tempered when I started out next day for the address in Surbiton supplied by Security. Surbiton has a reputation for money, but the map led away from the fatter houses and down comparatively packed and faulty streets. The slogans began, sprayed in red and black over walls and pavements: HIT AND RUN, ISLE OF MAN – BELSEN, YOU ARE A SHADOW OF YOURSELF, CUBA IS HOME, FLAMES ARE YOUR FRIENDS, HOWEVER YOU GO TAKE TEN OF THEM WITH YOU, YELLOW BROTHER-SUCKERS and the like.

From the outside the place looked like a tobacconist/newsagent for the down-and-out. The window was piled high with obsolete magazines. As I walked into the shop a bell buzzed loudly, operated by the doormat. There followed weighty footsteps on the stairs and in lumbered a man of about my size, with overgrown eyebrows and a straight mouth. His suit was too small for him and too thin for the climate. Metal-ended boots. He moved sideways until he was behind the counter, keeping his eyes on me all the time. I never saw anyone less like a shopkeeper or more like a Stone Age BG. The shop itself was unconvincing, its entire stock – motoring magazines, horse-lovers' gazettes, paperbacks about fishing and gardening, plus two shelves of old-fashioned cigarettes and only two brands of pot – wouldn't have raised more than two hundred quid. The man spoke slowly, with a murky accent.

'You have papers?'

'I didn't come to buy any papers. I was called here by your boss.'

He looked angry.

'No, your pass, certificate, clearances, identity.'

'If you want to see them,' I said slowly and precisely, 'you must ask me politely.'

'We are not playing Happy Families.'

'You may not be, but let me tell you that I'm Master Blood the Butcher's Son. I want respect and I get respect.'

'You are cheeky.'

This last was said very heavily, like a threat. So I sniffed up my snot and spat it on the floor.

'Lick it up,' he said.

By now I was sure he was an Afrikaaner. I've got nothing against them in general, but I didn't like this particular Boer. I looked at the ceiling until I'd got my next sentence loaded.

'I suppose you survived the massacre because you were a Kaffir's bum boy,' I said.

That was supposed to do it and that did it. He was halfway round the end of the counter when my right arm crunched round his neck. I jammed his stubble hard down on to *The Times*. Then I took control of his breathing. I let him use it now and again. I let him kick as much as he liked, those boots couldn't reach me. He didn't shout. Presumably he still thought he could grind me and he was too proud to be caught in a stranglehold by his employers upstairs. When I warned him gently that I now had the choice of either smashing his head against the floor or bending his spine until it snapped, he wisely stopped fighting. I removed his gun, gave him a neck-squeeze for luck and stood back suddenly so that he overbalanced, missed grabbing the electric light bulb by about four feet, and fell with his back in my spit-pool. One by one I produced my documents and held them in front of his face. I spoke slowly, as if to an infant computer.

'This is my ID. This is my BG card. You will observe that my professional rating is first class, that the card is stamped with the word Honours and that it bears no endorsement for avoidable failure, panic, or any of the other ten faults. This one is my security clearance. You will see that it is edged with gold. You've probably never seen one like this before and I doubt if you ever will again. It means that as far as state security goes, there is nowhere where I am verboten. Nowhere at all. The number on this card is very low. That does not indicate the order in which it was issued. It indicates a high trust rating even inside the gold. And this is a memo from Security asking me to come to this hopelessly transparent front of a shop. You reckon you're a BG? They wouldn't trust you to clean the bog at Hollow Hill. You think you're under the protection of the Dutch Reformed God or something? Any five-year-old would spot this place as a fake. What fantastic security – a bloody buzzer stuck under the doormat.'

He was biting his lower lip. He knew it was all true, and he really seemed to regret it. It wasn't a case of carelessness, he seemed to care about what he was guarding. It was inexperience, lack of training, lack of respect and lack of horse sense. I decided to finish my lecture.

'And where's your cool? You were angry before I even spat on the floor. Do you walk around angry?'

'Yes.'

'Then get a wife and take it out on her, or bash a Kathead or a Spieler, or jack off under the counter while you look at the photos in *The Zulu Motorist*. You've got all that anger, well you can't help that. But don't bring it to work with you.'

'You spat on our territory.'

'I spat on the floor.'

'You spat on our land.'

'If you want to end your life as a pub fighter, OK, I spat on the floor and the floor doesn't feel spit and the floor is not a land or a territory. A floor is just a floor. There is a law of gravity, even where you come from. If I spit, the spit goes downwards towards the centre of the earth – unless I spit straight in your eye. If you think that a floor is anything more than a floor, I suggest that your thinking is trash. Are you all the security this place has got?'

'Two of us work shifts.'

'Well your boss is a gambler. Even if I was running this place as a straight shop I'd want more precautions than you've got. This is England, not bloody China you know.'

He nodded, he'd had enough. I gave him back his pistol, barrel first, watching his eyes, signalling that if he tried to turn it on me I'd be there to meet him promptly with my own pet gun. He grinned for the first time as he dropped it back under his armpit. His thoughts were easily legible. He was obviously going to have to take orders from me in the future, so he'd decided to change down and do a grovel.

Slivers of old brown wood were fraying from the stairs, there was no carpet. Six-year-old cream paint shed dandruff from the walls. At the top was a door with an authentic slide-back peep-hole. Inside the room thick green blinds which looked as if they'd never again be raised were drawn tight down to the window ledges. The floor sported the skin of a zebra. One wall was dominated by a six foot high map of Africa, portraits of hand-coloured Boers and a row of metal filing-cabinets. Behind a table sat three old crab-apple white men attended by a girl with polystyrene skin who might have been a secretary or a night nurse. The old man on the left was phoning. He looked up at me, made a face at the receiver and said to it:

'Get off the line, we have company.'

He hung up.

I said: 'Don't bother about me. I'm sure you can talk as freely in front of me as you can to the phone-tapping corps.'

None of them liked that. As a cutting witticism or a piece of showing off I didn't like it either, but I'd seen enough child-ishness about security for one day. I decided to turn diplomat, taking out my credentials and placing them gently, face up-wards, on the table. The three wise men shunted them back and forth amongst themselves until the one in the centre, whom I recognized, shuffled them together, grunted and pushed them back. He cleared his throat at me.

'We are the South African Government in Exile.'

'I'm honoured to meet you. I've admired your courageous struggle for a long time, Doctor.'

The central crab-apple nodded, but did not smile.

'We need your help,' he said. 'We've lost most of our best people. Night and day we are under threat.'

'Who's threatening?'

'We get letters. Some are signed in blood.'

His left-hand crab-apple slid open a drawer packed with letters, then tapped it shut again.

'Black Africa has riddled Britain with her agents. And yet you lecture us about security...'

'Well, bet on it that no black agent's going to get within seventy miles of Surbiton. They're either in the ghettoes or undergoing rehabilitation.'

'You understand that we also have many white and almost-white enemies. You have heard of crypto-whites, Mr Rossman? Since the Black Africans began the War of Attrition, and especially since the massacres, our people have been tracked down and persecuted in every country on earth.'

'I thought the war was over.'

He stood up. I had gone too far. He spoke very slowly.

'The – war – is – never – over. We are not powerless, Mr Rossman, we are not political eunuchs. But there are many who would like to see us dead and stuffed.'

'Surely Black Africa's got enough troubles of its own without messing around with revenge killings over here?'

'Not revenge, Mr Rossman. Prevention. There are whites still alive in Africa. And some of them are cunning enough or lucky enough to remain free. In some areas. Add to them the immense, dissatisfied armies of blacks who now find that they are not automatically presented with a Cadillac, a state-financed skyscraper of their own and a brothel full of white women.

There are many, many people on the African continent, Mr Rossman, who are panting for our return.'

'And Black Africa knows this?'

'So-called Black Africa both knows this and fears this. And I omitted to mention that there are many powerful white nations who have given their promises to support our return to our rightful homeland. To the hilt, Mr Rossman.'

The crab-apple on the doctor's left added:

'And when the sword goes in, it will go in to the hilt.'

The doctor said: 'You think we are romantics. Very well. We are not obliged to offer you proof. But you will see proof of our will and our strength.'

'I'm bound to believe you. All I know is that your security system has dry rot.'

'Precisely. That's why we hired your services, Mr Rossman.'

'I'll need another BG to work with.'

'We have already—'

'You've already got a commissionaire if you mean that goon. I need a Hollow-Hill trained BG I can work with. Give me a couple of days and I'll report back here with a partner.'

The doctor nodded. I grinned and left. On a job like this I needed an assistant. If you're not in the game yourself, this might seem like a joke. Who will guard the bodyguard, bodyguard guard thyself, and all that. No joke. You need a trusty sidekick partly for when you have to sleep, partly to act as longstop if you're hit, partly to work with you as a scrum half works with a scrum, and partly to learn from you as an apprentice. And partly, I'll admit it, for your own protection. But last things last.

When I put round word I wanted an assistant, twenty applied and I arranged to see them all. I sat behind a desk caressed by the breeze from a rubber-bladed fan. In the outer office, on the stairs and along the street, lay an overweight heat-wave. One by one they paraded in, the big, sweating men, and I watched as the electric gusts dried their sweat and I smiled as they began to shiver. Most of them could have done the job well enough, but I wanted more, I wanted everything from them and magic as well. Define that? Magic, I don't know what else to call it, the twin signs in a man's eyes which mean brilliance, which don't only advertise quickness, strength and reliability, but also announce – SPECIAL. I didn't see that in the first ten, merely a procession of men with oversize fists, mostly clenched with tension. Jarmyn was the eleventh to come in. He looked at me for a second, spent another second looking round the room, then looked at me again and nodded. I laughed. It was one of those double laughs, relief and disbelief combined. I couldn't say anything for staring at him. He stood there, seriously, about five foot eight, slim, black hair curled all over his head and halfway over his ears, eyes slanted and slightly hooded, nose with delicate lines turning up slightly at the end, mouth small, only one ear showing and that ear pointed at the top, hands loose at his sides with long fingers, light-blue silk suit and those white leather shoes, body balanced so finely, Christ, a bloody dancer. He was not sweating. He was the wrong shape, wrong size, wrong features, but the twin signs were in his eyes, he had the magic. I told him to sit down and watched how he did it. There is a skill even in sitting down, there is an art in everything the body can do.

I said: 'They liked you at Hollow Hill.'
'Yes. Their standards could be higher.'
'They're the best in the world.'
'Sure. I wasn't comparing them with the rest of the world.'
'Why are you a BG?'
'I'm a bodyguard—' I began to wonder if he was as quick as all that, his answers could have fewer words in them, he shouldn't need time to think what he was going to say, he shouldn't have to rephrase the question like that – 'because it makes sense. I worked plainclothes with subverts' – I nodded to assure him that I had read his references and his right eyelid flickered as he took the hint not to waste any time on his record

– 'and I hate subverts. And I always knew I could be one of the best bodyguards in the world. It doesn't tense me up to concentrate for hours at a time. I don't daydream. My eyesight's exceptional. I can see details other people don't see.'

It didn't sound rehearsed, but he might be a cool actor. His voice was odd, odd like an alto sax, it hit me that it was a beautiful voice roughened at the edges. I liked his words too, they seemed open and clean to me. I was conscious of being magicked by some tough charm which he seemed unaware of. I had to backtrack.

'Tell me why you hate subverts.'

'Because they carry chaos in their heads. I like order. Control.' He smiled a controlled smile. 'And I love England.'

'What England?'

'Very complicated. There's a village I go to in Yorkshire. People meet in the pub, farmers, shopkeepers, the local carpenter, me, the doctor, we lean against the bar and things are easy between us. Maybe we decide to play football, so we play football. Or I may decide to keep to myself, avoid the pub and walk up on to the moors—'

'Then why don't you live there?'

'Didn't finish. I like that, but I like the city too. Because in the city you can forget all that neighbour stuff. Nobody has to be friends. You're competing, you're struggling, you're using your eyes and your brain and your body. Nobody's equal, ever, in the city. Any city is just a series of little battlefields. Win or lose. I like that. And I don't want either the city or the country to change. Yes, that's why I hate subverts.'

He was trying to use the language, trying to fog me with words. I tried to catch him off balance.

'What animal are you?'

'Bit of a hawk and bit of a crocodile.'

'Where's your mother?'

'She's dead.'

'What do your closest friends do?'

'They puzzle their heads about me.'
'Think of one man.'
'Myself.'
'Think of another.'
'Commander Gray.'

I laughed, this time because Gray was in my head when I asked Jarmyn to think of a man. And that had been the point of trying to throw him, to see if we could bust through to an instant telepathy or simply sympathy. We'd done it in record time. I threw an ashtray at him, not too hard. He caught it and threw it back, I ducked and it dented the wall behind me. He was certainly quick, he was certainly not afraid.

'Why did you throw it back?'
'People throw things at me, I throw them back harder.'
'Yeah, but you're being interviewed. Trying to get a job with me.'
'I don't have to take any shit from you.'

And I liked that.

'All right,' I said. 'You ask me questions.'
'What bothers you?'
'Inefficiency.'
'What do you do when you detect inefficiency?'
'First, I correct its results as quick as I can. Next I find out why it happened. Next I make sure it can't happen again. Now I'll ask you some more questions, Jarmyn. Any dependants?'
'None.'
'What do you do for sex life?'
'I buy it.'
'Why? Can't you get it free?'
'No, it's never free. I could get it without paying money, but that way you're in danger of paying emotion and once you start doing that you can get trapped in it. Hire purchase. I like to work alone and live alone.'
'You enjoy your own company?'
'It suits me. I don't bore myself.'

'That's good.'
'It's deliberate.'
'When could you start?'
'Any time.'
'Why'd you leave your last target? His reference says that you're inclined to be headstrong.'

'Yes, it would say something like that. I left because I gave him essential advice and he wouldn't take it. I warned him against a place where he mustn't go and he went. He tried to shake me off twice to get there. I reckoned he wanted to be gunned. I don't work for suicides. So I resigned.'

'That was five weeks ago and you haven't worked since.'

'A little casual work for the Yellows. Strictly for cash. I was waiting for the right job.'

'You've got it. Get out to the waiting-room and tell those monsters to go home.'

His mouth lengthened. He said:

'One thing. I take orders and I take them fast. On duty. But off duty we're both the same size. I know that's not usual. Most big BGs want a crawler, not an assistant. But I know how I work. And I work best that way.'

'You talk well.'

'I work better.'

'All right, Jarmyn, you won't have to take any shit from me. Now will you tell the rest of them to go home?'

He got up and went out and got rid of them. With Jarmyn, I spent a week caulking all the leaks at Surbiton. We brought in the biggest of the security firms, who laid down a labyrinth of alarms, installed the standard iron door, proofed the windows – one of them had to be bricked up – and spiked off the rooftop. They also cut an emergency exit behind the doctor's desk which, to give him credit, was Jarmyn's idea. Altogether it cost about a thousand, plus a maintenance contract, but the South African Government in Exile (SAGE) could afford that. When the fleet of white refugee ships poured out of South Africa, they bulged with gold and black prisoners. Naturally the white exiles wanted to retain their identity in an England of wet-dream culture and menacing weather, so they clubbed together, bought a tract of Surrey countryside, mowed down the silver birches and built their own city, compact and gleaming, with squat white towers, ditched around, walled around and wired about. Always referred to as New Johannesburg, it published its own newspapers, magazines and books, ran its own radio and education machine. You needed a visa to get in and out. (The shop in Surbiton, it turned out, was no more than a somewhat secretive Embassy.) Most of the time the doctor spent in New Johannesburg, planning strategy in the twenty-four-hour War Room, receiving deputations, awarding honours, broadcasting to his people and so on. At first Jarmyn and I felt uncomfortable in the place. Afrikaans was the official language. But that wasn't the only foreign feeling. I've never before been in a city where the Head of State could stroll along the street in daylight, accompanied only by two BGs and stop casually to talk to groups of shoppers. And there were so few policemen visible. Of course there were uniformed cops, but they were either checking entry and re-entry at the gates or sorting out the eternal queues of American cars in the streets. We were reassured by the doctor.

'In New Johannesburg every man, woman and child is a policeman. At twelve they are trained to use guns. At sixteen they are trained in all aspects of warfare. Every household has its own armoury. We are an army. We are also, in case you hadn't noticed it, a civilization.'

Jarmyn, who had been enthusiastically approved by the doctor after a brief interview, said:

'I understand only so far. You've got a civilization of your own. You keep it tidy, you keep it in quarantine from the corruption outside and I'm sure you're right about that. And you keep this civilization geared for armed struggle—'

'And that struggle will come soon. When we return.'

'Of course, Doctor. But in the meantime, and I don't suppose you'll be able to launch the invasion for, well say ten years—'

'That depends very much on the attitude of the European Community,' said the doctor. 'If they had the will to burn away the corruption of their own peoples, once and for all, then they could turn to us. With their help we could return to our homeland tomorrow.'

I said: 'There are plenty of us fighting The Rot, sir. But in England it's not always easy to pinpoint the subverts.'

Jarmyn said: 'But the doctor's right. I've always said so. The chainwork should be a hell of a lot tighter. Or we'll go down. But can I get back to business, Doctor? A civilization geared for armed struggle. What sort of frustration builds in that civilization when the day of judgement seems so far away?'

The doctor gave us his antique smile.

'Frustration is very serious. I take it very seriously. The militant frustration of which you speak is being satisfied. Many of our young men volunteer for service with either the Yellows in Europe or the American forces fighting in South America. They are attached for limited periods and they acquit themselves well. Our stay-at-homes, well, they can always visit the Zoo.'

We laughed.

'I said: 'I'm not bothered personally, Doctor. But what do you do about sexual frustration in the city? I mean, not you yourself, but your people. I mean, you've got surprisingly strict anti-pornography and anti-adultery laws. Aren't you inviting violence if there's no kind of outlet?'

The doctor didn't answer me then. But we soon found out. Every other day Jarmyn and I would spend an hour or more waiting in the ante-room of the doctor's 'club'. Waiting. It's a funny thing, but if I'm off duty and waiting for a friend, I'm just like anyone else, following the second hand of my watch, rereading the same story in the newspaper without understanding it, getting annoyed about other people's lack of precision. But that's in my own time. Duty's different. Professional waiting is not boring, at least you must keep telling yourself that and in the end you believe it. Because a bored BG is a dead BG. Before I wait, I always insist that my target or his aide should make it absolutely clear where I am supposed to wait. Then I take up my post and I rivet my feet to the floor. My concentration may become ruffled, my pocket snack of cold toasted cheese sandwich may seem a poor exchange for the pink-lit steak being consumed beyond the plate-glass by my target, perfumes may taunt me, but I will not be moved by anything less than a bulldozer. The bull in the Spanish ring chooses his special piece of territory, his safe place. So do I. In my imagination I construct an invisible cube, about the size of a telephone box. I look around, I step inside and then I occupy it. That cube of air is mine. If anyone threatens to overstep its edges, my eyes say: 'Keep Out.' My eyes are obeyed by ninety-nine people out of a hundred. Within this cube I can even, after my own fashion, relax.

The doctor's 'club' was, to put it bluntly, an executive brothel. It was an impeccably reliable machine, confined to SAGE's inner circle. (There were lesser clubs for the rest of the male population.) The girls themselves, none of them South African, were subject to regular medical inspections and security clearances. The club contained not only sexual amenities, but also a swimming-pool and a cinema which showed little else but old South African travelogues.

The ante-room of the 'club' was also its bar, and it was here that the doctor assigned us to wait. Around the chandeliered room, on red velvet settees with belly-buttons, the girls, a chummy bunch, awaited their guests. The bar was high, padded, and with a top which overhung the brass footrail by about ten inches. Behind the bar, Madame was usually in attendance, slim for her years and with remarkably illuminated eyes. I rapidly entered her good books, and while always refusing the services of Madame while on duty, I thought it good policy to visit the club on my own account several times on my half-days. Madame was a jealous woman, and so, although I exchanged banter with the girls, I was always at pains not to favour any particular one of them. On duty, I would stand in my transparent cube at the bar, Jarmyn would take a settee and read one of an endless series of government publications. I would accept the occasional whisky from Madame, with an equal amount of water, but I would stay in my safe place until my target was ready to leave. Madame certainly respected me for this, she told me so, though I cannot speak for the girls, who were certainly less duty-conscious and exchanged many a joke about my physical bulk. I knew there was a spark of provocation behind these jokes, but I pretended that I didn't. There was one girl in particular, called Jenny, wide-mouthed and indefatigably gabby, who dropped hints to me which became heavier and heavier, more like bricks. I tried to make my position, security-wise and Madame-wise, clear to her as tactfully as possible. I wasn't after Jenny anyway. I wasn't after that sort of thing at all. But Jenny persisted. She was clearly no nymphomaniac, but without meaning to I had aroused some imp in her body. In the end she turned angry and vowed to 'get me anyway'.

A week after that threat I was waiting for the doctor in my usual place. Madame, after watching him disappear with one of the sturdier girls, poured me a double Scotch. I nodded a greeting to the three girls on settees. Jenny was not among them. Jarmyn, with a fat paperback called *New Strategies in Riot Control*, was doggedly educating himself. I admired his concentration, but I have always believed in learning from life, not books.

Madame touched my chin, which retains minute stubble no matter how often I shave. (They keep introducing new improved razor blades, but I can never use one blade more than three times, however improved. Electric razors are no use on stubble like mine.) Madame, as they say in the courts, had been drinking but was not drunk, as I noted when she began to tell me, for the second time, about the year and a half which she spent training as an opera singer under a sexual maniac named Oscar Floreur. (The State, over the past ten years, has spent more money on encouraging opera than anyother country in the European Community. I have been a few times, but I think you have to be a regular.) Madame's voice was full, it reminded me of an open tin of peaches, and I enjoyed it as much for its music as for what it was saying.

'Floreur,' she said, 'was besotted by my body from the start. During my second lesson he put his arm round my shoulder, propelled me violently towards the middle of his curtained bow window, strode away from me like a melodramatic robot, shook his head from side to side until I heard his neck click disconcertingly, sat down at his baby grand, played three chords and then said: "That's what you're doing to me, Mercia." I ignored all this. He said, "Haven't you heard of ragged chords. That is what you do to my poor nervous system, all the way down." I laughed, "Ha ha ha." He pulled at his hair rather crudely and said that he couldn't go on. I said my parents were paying for me to be taught to sing. He said yes, he was constantly aware of my parents, especially my mother, but did I want only my voice to sing? By this time I was playing with him, more or less, mentally I mean, so I said: "With what else should I sing?" He said, "Every part of you should sing, your eyes should sing, your cheeks should sing, your neck should sing, your shoulders should sing, your breasts should be chanting together, your back should be trembling with music, your ribs, each of your perfect xylophone ribs should vibrate, your umbilical whirlpool should, your belly should, your clitoris, your quim, oh Jesus Mercia, your legs, the lovely long strings of your legs, your feet should be singing round behind me somewhere." At this point he folded up in the middle and hid his face on his forearms. My heart kept saying – come on then, let's fuck – but I knew I couldn't say that; I just touched his cheek like this and kissed his eyes like this and as he looked up, you know, Rossman, he was crying.'

She was crying, too. But I could see, in the mirror behind her, that my face had become a mask carved out of scrubbed pinewood. Jenny was getting me. In full view of the other three girls and Jarmyn, but concealed from Madame by the overhanging bar, she had crawled the length of the bar into my transparent cube during the soliloquy. As I stood there, testing myself like the Spartan boy with a fox up his jumper, her hand had unzipped my flies, had extracted my person and was moulding it into stern life. I looked down, showing the lower range of my teeth like Bogart, giving Jenny the 'Keep-Out' message. Madame had poured me another drink, and this one went straight down. Immediately I'd drunk it I regretted not showering it over Jenny. I flashed a second 'Keep Out'. But Jenny was already in; she raised a sooty eyebrow and opened her lips wider. Then she folded them around me again. Madame continued:

'Floreur,' she said, 'had thought I was a virgin, in fact I think he was afraid that every woman in the world was a virgin. He would look at them and listen to their conversation, and from their modesty in not wearing topless costumes on every occasion and their chastity in not using obscenities in a chat about the weather – well there are girls like that you know, my dear Rossman, you just say to them: "Hope it doesn't rain, dear," and they reply: "It's going to piss down, my arsehole's as tight as the Pope's X-fronts" – anyway, because they don't all roll on their back and play Danish open sandwich at the first touch of Schubert, Floreur used to think he was the only creature with any sexual impulse left on the planet earth.'

Jenny's tongue was now concentrating on the underside of my person's shaft. That tongue found the valuable blue vein which runs down the lower side. She crouched, rather uncomfortably I'd have thought, supporting herself with one hand, while the other hand was treating my gonads as though they were a glass of brandy. One second I was inside her mouth, her teeth playing arpeggios all around me, and the next moment I was out in the open air and aching, against my will, to be vacuumed back.

Madame poured me another drink and swigged her own. The red lines in her eyes were beginning to light up.

'There was no stopping Floreur,' she said. 'He wanted to give up music for what he called the total music of my body. A man prepared to abandon the world, at least his world as a music teacher, in order to devote himself to the worship of little Mercia. Some religion, you may well say, but he was devout. Devout. They broke the mould when they made him,' she said.

'There's not many men,' I said as loudly as seemed reasonable, as I wanted to drown out the slurping sounds which Jenny and I seemed to be making. 'There's not many men who take love as seriously as that.'

'You're right, my Rossman, you're so fucking right,' shouted Madame, pulling my head across the bar and nose-diving it into her bosoms. I thought of Jenny, mining down below, head almost crushed, luckily for her into the plush lining of the bar, by my heavier-than-average thighs. But Jenny was soldiering on and by now she had to go on and one of my hands was below the bar, my left hand it must have been because my drink was in my right, my left hand, pressing her head down on me, trying to impale her, pressing out the rhythm on her midnight curls. And feigning drunk, or at least a little drunk, I tried to conceal my movements by singing in rhythm with my body's rhythm, my words muted and lost between the breasts of Madame, and that is how I came into Jenny's mouth, half-supported by the bar, half by Madame's breasts, one leg in the air. I raised my head and saw in the mirror that the other girls were pretending to laugh at a cartoon in a magazine as I spurted and spurted. Jarmyn was reading.

It has occurred to me since that Madame may have been in on the joke. But I don't think that could be true. The doctor certainly wasn't. From the doorway he stared, turned red, and nodded to me to put myself away doublequick. He could have sacked me, but he didn't, in fact he never mentioned the incident. But he never took me to the club again and I never went there on my own after that. And don't get the wrong idea. Most of the duty waiting I've done has been less eventful. Four hours standing on a marble floor and nothing but a fawn-tiled pillar to lean against is more like the day-to-day routine of yours faithfully, I'm happy to say.

I like routine. Jarmyn, I sensed, was only in the business for those short bursts of action in which he could explode. He was an explosive man in the sense that he was a fanatic for politics. I have never been a fanatic about anything except for the pattern and details of my profession. I'm not afraid of explosions of action, but I don't carry a torch for them. I do not even hate The Rot, I recognize it for what it is, a force against which I coldly oppose my body and my mind and my will and my skill.

Much of my time with the SAGE was spent in New Johannesburg. But there were excursions. It was necessary for the doctor to make occasional tours, lecturing to select groups about the future of Africa, acting as a lobbyist at European Community Headquarters in Bonn. I respected the doctor and he reciprocated. He always had the decency to show me his projected programmes and routes, and would usually respond affirmatively to my suggestions. I even initiated a couple of successful contacts. Jarmyn, to his credit, never tried to push himself. If he had suggestions, and he sometimes had good ones, he would pass them through me to the doctor.

Each week, on Saturday, we would visit the Zoo. Occasionally we would go on a Monday and Wednesday as well in a slack week, but the doctor never missed a Saturday. The Zoo could only be reached through New Johannesburg, and security was fierce. There were no animals in the Zoo, but many cages. In the cages were black South Africans of various shapes and sizes. On my first visit I understood exactly what the doctor meant about the answer to frustration. For the exhibited blacks were freely available to anyone who carried a Zoo Pass. It was a serious playground, and the blacks were the toys. What you did with them was up to you. You could feed them, with whatever you liked. You could order them to perform whatever tricks you fancied. You could simply take photographs (they were all naked). You could walk into a den containing one, two or a whole family of them, carrying only a whip, and get down to business. You could select one for questioning, take him or her to a fully-equipped interrogation room, and play question and answer to your heart's content. An exile VIP could become a surgeon for the day, choose his patient and, under the supervision of an expert, perform any series of experiments. Electrodes, scalpels, kidney-bowls, tape-recorders, operating tables, dental equipment – everything was free. There were deaths, of course, but the Zoo was well stocked. The only rule about the treatment of an exhibit was that no visitor should have even tentative sexual relations with it. I believe that this was hard to enforce. The prohibition did not, of course, apply to a visitor who ejaculated involuntarily while performing surgery. Naturally I didn't participate in these activities. My role did not extend beyond restraining recalcitrant exhibits for the doctor.

I would hate to give the wrong impression about the Zoo. It should be borne in mind that these exhibits were not selected at random. They were all subverts or the children of subverts. Most of them, even among these irrevocable offenders, appeared happy as they scampered round their cages or begged through the bars. It is of course stupid to generalize about anything, even grass, but I would like to say from my observations in the Zoo that your average black subvert is child-like, servile and cowardly by inclination. Recently Jarmyn showed me a book in which it is proved that their nerves are coated with an extra lining of tissue, so that a pain which would seem unbearable to a white man is, however much he protests, more tolerable to a black. I should also point out that the Zoo keepers, or those whom I met, were, to a man, conscientious professionals with a keen sense of humour.

Altogether I was contented in my work for the SAGE and began to look forward, almost as keenly as a down-home Afrikaaner, to the Return. But all good things come to an end, and after a year under the doctor, Security suggested that I should move on, leaving Jarmyn as my successor. Jarmyn organized my farewell party, a warm occasion. The drinks were served by the Boer bodyguard I'd first met in that murky, inauspicious shop in Surbiton. He seemed to bear me no resentment.

My new target was Sir Arthur Monkton-Jones. Security impressed me with his eminence as a scientist, but when I asked for a list of his publications so that I could background him before we met, there was a silence as if I'd thrown an egg at the wall. Security looked at me from behind tobacco-flecked spectacles and finally said:

'He hasn't published anything for about fifteen years, but I expect you'll have seen him on television.'

I could have bitten my head off. Of course I'd watched him on panel games about sport, on women's afternoon shows explaining how he intended to spend his birthday, talking about economics and social order on topical programmes and chatting with clean-looking actresses about old films late at night. It was just that I'd allowed the fact that he was a scientist to be sunk by the super-powered rubber ball of his public personality, all those pink photos of him in the gossip columns and the affectionate magazine descriptions of his 1950s style clothes (he admitted to being a 'Teddy Boy' in the old days). I suppose he was a man's man because of the cleft in his chin and those woolly eyebrows, but also a woman's man because of his open-air gentility. He had three hundred and twenty proposals of marriage a week by repute, and since at least twenty of these must be from acceptable women, were he unscrupulous it might have been possible for him to marry twenty women in one week. Over a year that would amount to more than a thousand brides.

I chuckled at the thought, then braked my amusement. Security was staring at me.

'I know he's very much in the public eye, sir,' I said, 'but I wouldn't have thought he'd be very high on The Rot's death list.'

Security plonked a copy of *The Times* under my nose. MONKTON-JONES TO SPEAK FOR SCIENCE, SAYS PM.

'You won't be lolling about outside laboratories with chemical smells up your nose,' said Security. 'Mainly studios and public appearances of all sorts. Don't be fooled at first. Monkton-Jones is popular now and up till this morning nobody had any reason to put him in their sights. This headline changes all that. He's had ten years' fun as intellectual cheesecake, we looked after that, saw him right you understand, ten years of champagning blondes and cooing to the millions. Stateroll's given him mass money and mass love. Now he's about to earn it, start real work, buckle down and pay off.'

'Explaining State policy on science? He'll have a lot of secrets then, defence stuff, germ development, orbital missile chainwork and all that.'

'We wouldn't let him run around loose if he carried secrets. No, he'll announce new developments in science, but they won't be all that new. Nothing that China hasn't known for a few years anyway. But these things will have been secrets to the public. It's important to use a sympathetic salesman on a product like this.'

It was beginning to add up, so I nodded, waited for Security to hand me a slim file, and left.

Sir Arthur's house was surrounded by a small pine wood, then the trees gave way to sandy soil and grass, and an artificial lake, obviously artificial because its waters were a deep blue, and there in the middle of the lake was the most beautiful construction I have ever seen in my life. At first it seemed to be an iceberg of curves and crags and rough and smooth textures, but it was a house, an iceberg house, and we had to take a semicircle round the lake to reach a rough curving bridge of pure white cement. Sir Arthur's chauffeur, almost as tall as me, led the way from the car, but I paused on the bridge, looking at the chemically blue water and those young pine trees and it seemed good to me, it seemed quite different from anywhere, and my throat suddenly seemed to be full of the bricks of my boyhood streets, bricks crammed together, people crammed together as close as the bricks, held together by an awful cement of tension. The grime of that city, and the abrupt shapes of that city, and the way in which that city had no shape itself so that even after living in it for fifteen years I could get lost by daylight, because it had no landmarks you see, even the church spires were identical, there was no river, no port, a flat town in a hollow in the earth of the Midlands with a brown colour in the air and over the pavements, brown dust along the pavements as if the bricks were powdering in the dull wind. I never could have expressed or understood its ugliness then, I could only sense it, I could never have said, even to myself, this city is a machine for grinding and degrading men, no I could never have said it, but I sensed it, and sometimes, in my adolescent way, I would cry for that city and not just for myself in that city but for the others, and for the sake of the earth that had been despoiled so that such a foul maze of grit in your eye and early darkness could be erected, where the greatest tug of romance came from the movies and from the posters saying JOIN THE ARMY and where you only came of age when they'd serve you in the pubs so you could drink until you didn't care about that deadening city any more and maybe then go out with some friends and wreck some little part of the city, a phone box or a row of milk bottles or the windows of an old scowling chapel.

Did you often think about this? Did you often see it like that?

I saw it like that when I was a kid. I saw it like that when I first saw that iceberg-island house. And I saw it just now, when I was talking about it.

And in between those times?

It was something to forget. There are some things I like to remember about when I was a boy. Like the time the first men landed on the moon. The way they stood on that place, those two men. The way they talked to each other. I wish I could hear them talking on the moon again, those first men.

There's a tape of what they said. I'll get it for you. You can play it as much as you like. You'd better sleep now. Tomorrow you can dictate some more about Sir Arthur.

Good morning. It is morning, isn't it? Thanks a lot for the tape, the nurse brought it this morning. It is morning isn't it?

Yes. Good morning. You had just arrived at Sir Arthur's house, you remember?

Yes. That house. I knew before I met Sir Arthur that I'd like him, because even if he turned out to be cold and hard like the iceberg house, at least he'd made it possible for me to see that water among the sand and pines and that unmeltable iceberg. Unmeltable barring a particularly bad war, of course. He was upstairs in a roughly oval shaped tower with curving windows which looked beyond the trees, frames on the wall containing electronic pictures which glowed deeply, changing slowly, rough white furs under my suede shoes and a weakish handshake with the skin on his hand too loose for my liking. Then I stepped back. Sir Arthur relaxed, or it could be collapsed, into an egglike chair. His staff posed around him, one taking notes, one in the act of pouring him a drink, one fiddling ineptly with a machine which might have been a tape-recorder or a pocket TV or a weapon for that matter. Sir Arthur didn't look up at me, or rather he didn't look at my eyes, focusing on my belt. But I could see that his eyes were an even brighter blue than when they appeared on TV.

He said: 'I don't want to be rude, but I'm not sure what your duties will be. I'm not even sure that I need a bodyguard. I didn't ask for one.'

I said: 'They tell me that you'll need a BG. The Rot seems to be spreading fast at the moment. Nobody in a big Stateroll job is safe. I've met these boys, sir, I've dealt with them too. Good many of them are nuts.'

'But I'm merely going to be a spokesman.'

'A very valuable spokesman, sir.'

His mouth looked bitter. He drank and suddenly his talk turned wild, as if he'd been scorched by the drink.

'Once upon a time I was a valuable *scientist*, not a valuable *government* scientist, because I was finding out truth, you know, tearing the skin, all the layers of skin off and finding the real bones you understand, then grinding down the bones and there it was, in powder form, the truth. And that powder was useful, Mr Rossman, very useful to people. It made them well, that sort of thing, you put it into ill people and it had the remarkable effect of making them better. There was a snag though. That powdered truth, your bonemeal truth stuff, there wasn't much money in it. In fact, to tell you the honest truth, there was danger in it.'

'What kind of danger?'

'Truth danger. Yes, you'll say, but what kind of truth is there that a government can't use? And it's a good question because almost every kind of truth can be twisted right around through one hundred and eighty degrees to serve any cause you care to name. But I wasn't working like an ordinary scientist, I was trying to bring all my methods and knowledge and skill, et cetera,' (and he said those words with a chill) 'to try to solve the problem of fear. The problem being that everyone I knew was afraid to some degree, much too afraid to be free, and why they were afraid and what could be done to cure that fear – that's what I was after. Years ago.'

'But you've been too busy.'

'I think I was too afraid. It was going right, my research, I was getting somewhere. That frightened me. I was spending my own money on that research too, I was getting poor. Poverty frightened me. The implications of what I was doing frightened me.'

'But surely that would be useful to any government, a cure for fear? Just slip it to your troops and police and withhold it from everyone else.'

'It wasn't turning out like that. It was turning out much too easily. It was too easy to make. I take it in a crude, diluted form.'

He lifted his drink to the light. It was golden but murky.

'Sir Arthur, I want to be frank.'

'It's good for you sometimes. Other times it's bad.'

'Sir Arthur, I've often heard you on TV. You talk more vividly in private.'

'You mean I sound more like a public relations man than a scientist? That's true. I'm out of the habit of talking with scientists.'

'Do you tell everyone about this courage drug or whatever it is? I've only just met you and if I didn't know your security rating I'd be on the phone to the Yellows before sunset.'

'I tell nobody outside my house. But this is my house. I never go out when I've been drinking this stuff.' He said the word 'stuff' very softly. 'Outside I've tried to forget that work, hide it away from myself and concentrate on money. The money came. I now have the most beautiful house in the world, I believe. That was all I wanted.'

'And a government job. You've got that too.'

'Yes. That I didn't want.'

'You could have turned it down.'

'No.'

Sir Arthur lowered his face into his hands and howled. His staff closed around him, touching his shoulders, looking at me coldly. I asked the way to my room, a bare and beautiful snow-cell, curving walls and windows of glass streaked with blue and orange. I sat down and typed a memo:

SPOTMEMO

From: Rossman
To: Security
Re: Target Monkton-Jones
1. Homed. Estate doublesafe.
2. Staffcheck starts tomorrow.
3. Target danger of self-kill.

I unpacked my code book and transmitter and sent that one over. Sir Arthur certainly looked like an imminent suicide to me. That made it a double job, and guarding a target from himself was no part of any Hollow Hill course. I soon found that I'd caught Sir Arthur in a rare mood. Outside his own home he would be sober and dominating, especially during his weekly visit to London to record his commentary for 'Science At Your Service', a Ministry show which plugged the achievements of Community scientists. In the twenty-four hours before recording, Sir Arthur would never drug or drink. The red lines would vanish from his eyes, his sentences would become clear and he would amble around the roof of his home, studying his Whitehall script. But as soon as we returned from one of these gigs, he would dive straight into the gold murk or the gin. There seemed little danger of his being bumped. Our London jaunts were made by different routes, at different times each week; we rarely stopped on our way to or from the BBC. (Only three people have been bumped in the last ten years in the TV Centre – every employee is trained in basic security techniques.) I checked Sir Arthur's personal staff, inside, outside and upside-down. I could fault one or two of them on minor points of political theory, as I understood it, but their devotion to my target, the main point, was cast in some indestructible metal I had never encountered before. They angrily defended every breath he took if I pushed them. Unanimously they believed that he spent the greater part of each day and night thinking about them and worrying about their future. That much they would tell me. But they were so savage in their loyalty that I couldn't press them to answer intimate questions. I even plotted until I'd laid his secretary though I didn't fancy her – a rather skinny girl – but even she supplied no revelations.

I took the danger of Sir Arthur's suicide very seriously. I combed his room for weapons. Strangely enough he had no gun. The house wasn't high enough for him to jump off the roof with any certainty and in any case his fall would be broken by the blue moat, which was not poisonous. (I tried a bowl of its water on a cat.) His supply of drugs baffled me. They weren't labelled but it was likely, I supposed, that some of them would be fatal if taken in sufficient quantities. Again, his staff were fanatical enough to help him die if he asked them. I knew one thing – the man had suicide in him. When he was on the border of incoherence, his talk was dominated by his own destruction or desolation. I made a note of some of his remarks, which I quote out of their rambling, hesitant context.

'I want to let my brain run so far that I can't follow it.'

'I kept waking up last night. Every time I went back to sleep I dreamt I was hit over the head with an iron bar. I must have been killed six or seven times last night.'

'Money is just a bloody cage.'

There were plenty of ordinary sentences too, mostly rational. But I became a collector of his more desperate exclamations. As soon as I'd filed enough I would pass them up the chainwork explaining that I thought Sir Arthur was in need of crash psychiatry. The last evening I spent with him was on the way home from London. We stopped at a local pub. Two masculine-feminine types ponced in and took up their stations on barstools side by side.

I said: 'Christ, bloody perves everywhere these days. It's a wonder we've got a birthrate.'

Sir Arthur was on his feet. He stared at me, face dead-white, mouth working silently. I followed him out. He said nothing as we drove home. He said nothing until we were both sitting in his study, facing each other.

'I want to tell you a story,' he said. 'Don't interrupt me or I'll throw my chair at your head. Five years ago, during the anti-Rot dragnet, a man and a woman were arrested. They didn't know each other and there was no connection between the two arrests. He was found guilty of sabotage and sent to a camp in Scotland. She'd been doing subvert propaganda in a big way. They put her somewhere in Cornwall. Both of them were unlucky enough to go to camps which contained surgical research units. He was used in a series of survival experiments. They systematically cut pieces off him and after each piece was cut off they would see how he got on without it. Lumps of skin, toes. They cut one of his balls off and saw he managed like that. Then they cut his other ball off. When they'd finished with him they let him hobble off. The woman was used in sex-change experiments. They cut off her breasts, sterilized her and pumped her full of male hormones. In the end they let her go too. Of course they have to report regularly. Somehow these two met, maybe through subvert friends, I don't know and I don't care how they met, but they met. They decided that it mattered tremendously that having found each other they must never lose each other. So they got married. Of course there's no sex about the marriage, but it was allowed. They're married. Those two in the pub.'

He was weeping, but he stared at me. He did not wipe away the tears.

I said: 'Can I go to bed now, sir?'

He whispered: 'That's a true story. I told it to you because I thought it might shake you up enough to change you from what you are. It shook me up.'

He looked away.

I said: 'I don't really understand, sir.'

'Go to bed.'

That night, about midnight, Sir Arthur's secretary came to my room. I reached out a lazy hand to part her dressing-gown. She produced an iron bar and bashed me across the side of the head, twice. Some time the next day the Yellows found me bound and gagged. They told me that Sir Arthur and his staff had defected and were thought to be well on their way to Black Africa. I'd like to listen to that tape of the men talking on the moon again now, please. Would you mind changing the spools? I'll doze a little while I listen.

+ I'm at the foot of the ladder + Although the surface appears to be very finely grained as you get close to it, it's almost like powder. Now and then it's very fine + There seems to be no difficulty in moving around as we suspected. + It's actually no trouble to walk around + We're essentially on a level place here – very level place here. + It looks like it's coming out nice and even. + OK, it's quite dark here in the shadow and a little hard for me to see if I have good footing. + Looks like it's a little difficult to dig through. + It's a very soft surface but + I run into a very hard surface, but it appears to be very cohesive material of the same sort. + It has a stark beauty all its own. It's like much of the high desert of the United States. It's different but it's very pretty out here. + You can really throw things a long way out here. + OK that's good. + I have no flags and I'm in minimum flow. + Looks good. + A good thought. + There you go. + Beautiful, beautiful. + Magnificent sight down here. Magnificent desolation. Both PLSSs normal on consumables. + It's hard to tell whether it's a cloud or a rock. Notice how you can pick it up. + Got to be careful that you are leaning in the direction you want to go, otherwise + Life support consumables still looking good. + Something interesting in the bottom of this little crater here. It may be ... Keep going. We've got a lot more. OK + I don't want to go into the sun if I can avoid it +

You do have to be rather careful to keep track of where your centre of mass is.

I must have gone to sleep.

You can sleep as much as you like.

I don't want to sleep too much. I want to get my story down. And, you know, in between times I want to play that tape. But I keep going to sleep.

The injections do that.

Can't I do without them? No, I can't. These wounds are a bit too real. I mean I can't feel them at the moment, but when I haven't had an injection for some time, then I begin to feel where the wounds are. Let's get on with the story, I want to get it down. I feel like talking again. Was I talking about my father?

No. You were just at the point where Monkton-Jones defected.

I'm not sure I'm getting everything in the right order. From the point of view of time.

That doesn't matter. We can sort it out later.

Yes. OK. Let's get it all down. I think that it was just after Monkton-Jones, yes, my church assignment. I'd better explain a few things first. Most BGs, at some time or another, find themselves on duty in a church, which may surprise you until you think about it. Your target may be an atheist or even a Buddhist, but he may well find it useful for socio-political reasons to make regular attendance at divine service. More significant still are those great meetings of targets – weddings and funerals – especially state funerals.

I remember one particularly interesting case of the geometrically progressing assassination. It worked like this. The ultimate object was to bump the Under-Secretary for Security. But this target was naturally the centre of a swarm of good BGs on the two or three occasions a year when he appeared in public. Most of these appearances were confined to military bases and other safe zones. So a double feint was plotted. First, the mistress of the Under-Secretary's brother was cornered by a stolen car while shopping in Oxford Street. She was beaten up quickly and thoroughly and tossed out of the car in Chelsea. As the Under-Secretary's brother, a man with private enterprise enemies of his own in the field of advertising, left her hospital after his second visit, he was gunned down. It then became clear that the beating had been a feint for the shooting and the Yellows concentrated on questioning all the corpse's business acquaintances. At his funeral, the Under-Secretary read the lesson, or rather half the lesson, for the reading-eagle from which he spoke was mined. Plastic. Eight killed, twenty-seven wounded.

Security is tighter these days. But a cathedral especially offers thousands of chances for the assassin. A BG whose target is to attend a service should note possible sniper nets in the architecture, be sure they are cleared, and glance over them every few seconds – the glint of metal shows up well against old stone. He should examine the Order of Service carefully so that he can be sure to rise to his feet a split second before his target and kneel one split second after him. Even in this age, targets tend to believe they are safer in a church than in a public house. The BG knows better. If a man is determined to kill, he's not likely to be prevented by some vague piety.

I have gone into the problems of the BG and Christian worship because my next important job was as BG to an archbishop. I was glad of this posting, which showed that Security had decided that the Monkton-Jones débâcle was not my fault and also because Church dignitaries tend to employ BGs trained by the Big Five Churches themselves – and a fine troop they are, quiet and dedicated men with a sense of tradition you could cut with a knife. But the archbishop, apparently, wanted fresh blood, he wanted the best and that meant hiring a Hollow Hill man. I can't say I'm entirely proud of my stint as an ecclesiastical BG, but I'd rather you judged my actions and told me if I could have done better.

The first two months of my employment were spent on the archbishop's yacht in the north-west Mediterranean. At no point was there any danger, and the huge, jovial archbishop might have been any rich holidaymaker as he reclined under the powerful sun, his yachting cap at a jaunty angle, a Rum Collins in one hand and *Time* magazine in the other. But when we returned to the palace, his whole way of life changed.

At home, the archbishop explained to me, he habitually wore his full regalia, toting his golden, jewelled shepherd's crook as casually as a commuter with an umbrella. In the basement, janitors were on duty night and day shovelling coke laced with incense into a small furnace which dispersed the syrupy smell of the mixture through brass pipes to every room. Small loudspeakers in corridors, rooms and lifts whispered appropriate music in a week-long cycle, including the *St Matthew Passion* and *The Messiah*. Enormous religious pictures sloped from every wall. They were not originals, for as the archbishop pointed out, all the best original holy paintings had been snapped up long ago by the Vatican and other concerns. No, they were reproductions, though to leave my description at that would be to do less than justice to the most amazing art treasures which have come my way. They were twice, or in some cases three times the size of the originals, and these 'blow-ups' were painted in a specially mixed paste-like substance so that they glowed not only in the dark but in the daylight or under neon strips. Here and there, on marbleized plinths, reposed bowls equipped with concealed lighting in which bones, toes, hair and other relics of the martyrs reposed in some preservative chemical solution. Narrow, simulated stone benches, decked with gargoyles, lined the sides of the palace's gigantic waiting-room, while the ceiling was a cinema screen on which was continually back-projected the movie of T. S. Eliot's *Murder in the Cathedral*. Every Sunday the Salisbury-bred chef supplied an iced cake resembling a different cathedral. There was a swimming-pool shaped like a cross.

As the massive archbishop showed me round, he appeared slightly self-conscious.

'I know what you're thinking, my son,' he said resonantly, 'you're thinking that a house in which *everything* smacks of religion must be lacking in *taste*. And if I am right in what you are thinking – you are correct. It is *tasteless*. It is *vulgar*. To put it in its kindest light, it is *over-insistent*. But what are the concepts of tastelessness and vulgarity in the context of a divinely ordered universe, the overwhelming wonder of a God who can steer the stars through their enormous orbits and yet discern the past, present and future of the humblest electron? Vulgar-shmulgar as our Hebrew friends would put it – I want the whole universe to declare the glory of God, I want every tree and stone and animal to bear witness to *Him* and what I've done here is just a tentative swipe in that direction. Do you like it?'

I said that I liked it. I agreed to his suggestion that I should wear a monk's habit, so long as I could equip it with pockets for the tools of my trade. I said to him that, as a man of God, the necessity of having a bodyguard must seem inappropriate and even irksome. He replied as follows:

'No, dear child. Remember that Jesus Himself surrounded Himself with twelve BGs. Most of them were fishermen. Now let's consider *that*. In my experience the professional fisherman is husky, has patience and can react instantaneously after long periods of inaction. Fishermen are also used to working in teams – net fishermen I mean. (I would suspect a bodyguard who said his *hobby* was fishing. This would imply patience, to be sure, but not teamwork, quite the reverse, it would imply *an urge to be alone*. Many anarchists are amateur fishermen.) So Our Lord was quite correct in choosing fishermen as his hard-core BGs. Then where did He make His Big Mistake – correction, His two Big Mistakes?

'First, He appears to have operated no internal security within His BG team. Doubting Thomas, who might well have been employed by Jesus as an *agent provocateur* among the disciples, certainly failed to provoke Judas into blurting out the secret of his treachery. Second, Jesus appears to have made the very basic mistake that, because He Himself was *financially under-motivated*, the same quality was shared by His BGs. So that Judas was probably turned into a subvert, not by personal antagonism or political turnabout, but simply by *lack of adequate remuneration*. Understanding Jesus as well as he did, Judas could not approach Him directly for money – that would be to invite an admonition in parable form and possible demotion. So the need for more money simply festered inside Judas until it broke out into betrayal. This is an extreme example of one broken line of communication between a target and his BGs. Now throughout history there have been cases in which BGs are supposed to have ganged up on their target and demanded pay rises, with threats of *physical violence*. If such a situation arose today, of course, the target would only have to make some promise in order to avoid immediate retaliation, and report the incident to the National Association of BGs. Disciplinary action, I am assured, would be immediate and effective. But Jesus, of course, lived before the days of the NABG. In His place I would have either made sure that my men were adequately paid, or, if this could not be squared with my anti-wealth statements, would have ensured that each man was willing to work for bed and board only, because of his religious conviction. I myself would prefer the former alternative. *Fanatics*, as we know only too well, are all too liable to explode.'

Whether the archbishop liked me or just liked talking, I didn't know, but our perambulations of the palace lasted about two hours, and we were passing a queue of hand-painted Michelangelo statues, when there was a slow clatter behind us. I whirled round and sidestepped to cover my employer and saw that a choir of about two hundred boys, women and men was forming up in lines of four, wearing scarlet robes with white fur trimmings and octagonal hats of a shining black material. At some signal which I missed, they began to whisper the Magnificat. The archbishop greeted them with an upraised hand, then indicated to me that we should continue our tour. The murmuring choir trailed behind us, their music apparently keeping time with our synchronized footsteps. My stomach felt alternately empty and full, my brain became weightless. I was high, and it was a smiling high.

We were progressing through a lofty library where a few bent-necked minor clergy bowed and closed their eyes in humility as we passed. The archbishop greeted each one with a cheery though silent manual benediction. Then a United Dairies milk bottle landed two yards from our feet and sprouted into flame. My gun was in my hand and I was round the back of the Roman History stack facing a forty-year-old woman with spectacles, hard lines on her face and a second petrol bomb in her fist. My two shots caught her in the chest and stomach and as she went down and the choir rushed forward, I grabbed the bomb, its fuse flaring, and hurled it through a stained-glass window featuring Joan of Arc in full hardware, while the archbishop swung his crozier mightily, smiting the assassin across the side of the chin eighteen inches before her face hit the floor. She was already dead as a couple of tenors and a contralto lined a book-trolley with *The Times*, lifted her on to it and wheeled her off towards the palace guardhouse for identification and disposal. Then our walk proceeded.

'They're so *bad* at it,' said the archbishop. 'So absurdly ineffective. The palace has a hundred doors, one can hardly guard them all the time, even with a choir of one hundred and eighty.'

I said: 'Excuse me, Your Grace, but you wouldn't even need to break in if you were a subvert. You'd only have to infiltrate that lot.'

I flicked my head backwards to indicate the choir. The archbishop stopped and scratched the back of his neck with the bloodied crozier. I passed him a handkerchief to wipe away the unseemly smear of red.

'Well they're all security-guaranteed,' he said.

'Who checks them?'

'Each one bears a clearance from the Ministry, a pass from the Yellows and a certificate from the Royal College of Music.'

He chuckled. I didn't.

'If you've got no subvert record you can get a low clearance from the Ministry and I could hustle you a Yellow pass within forty-eight hours in any cathedral city, given thirty quid and a pair of dark glasses.'

'Rossman, you're a man of the *world*. What would you do if you were in my' – he seemed to be searching for the ecclesiastical word for them – '*shoes*?'

'Two things straight away, Your Grace. One, spot check right now. Two, in future always have the choir walk in front of you. I'll walk behind you.'

'The choir *in front* of me? But how would they knew where I wanted to go? I suppose I could shout commands. Or perhaps, more appropriately, I could *chant* them?'

'Why not, Your Grace?'

'And this, what did you call it, *spot check*?'

'Do it now, Your Grace. If there are any heavy subverts in that lot, they'll know that a new BG from the Hill means danger. By tomorrow they'll have had time to cache their weapons and they'll lie low till they find out if I make any difference. We've got to search them right away.'

He looked upwards, lowered his eyelids for a second, then looked me severely in the eyes.

'My son,' he said, 'we will spot check.'

He turned to the choir and motioned them into silence.

'Children,' he said, 'you will follow me.'

He took a brisk right turn and I fell back to shepherd the choir from behind. Nobody was going to drop out now. We entered a square courtyard alive with fountains and fantailed pigeons. Obedient to the gestures of the archbishop, the choir lined up in two puzzled rows across the cobblestones.

'My children. This morning we have seen a terrible example of the corruption which *riddles* these isles. A poor deluded woman, under our wondering eyes, changed into a monster. Don't worry about her, she had it coming, a beast in human shape, and a pretty peculiar shape at that.'

A pause of indulgence for giggles in the ranks.

'But now we must look to *ourselves*, look into our own hearts in an attempt to discover any further Judases, if Judases there be, among our serried ranks. I know this sounds silly, but I'm going to have to ask you to *strip off*.'

A soprano put up her hand.

'Your Grace, I'm not trying to be difficult, I'd just like to know. Do we have to strip completely?'

'Completely, *com-plete-ly*. Do not be ashamed, my daughter, of the body which God has seen fit to grant you. For your own safety, for my safety, for the safety of us all, until I am assured that not one amongst you carries the brand of Cain – *nobody leaves this courtyard!*'

As the choir began to struggle with the hooks and toggles of their robes, a bass voice began to chant, deeply and safely, the Twenty-third Psalm. One by one the other voices joined in, and as the scarlet-and-white robes fell to the cobbles and the choristers began to shed their assorted underwear, the sound of their singing swelled and soared.

The archbishop whispered to me: 'The Twenty-third is my *favourite*. And do you like the cobblestones? I purchased them in Lancashire for a *song*. Right. Now my son, I want you to search each and every one of these robes.'

So while I rummaged through the piles of robes, brassieres, pants, knickers, corsets, shoes and appliances, the archbishop glided up and down the ranks, trying to anticipate the identity of Judas from the expressions and bearing of his naked choristers. To do them credit, they stood there like bricks. I found cigarettes, matches, lighters, joints, handkerchiefs, combs, pencils, mirrors, string, make-up, marbles, fluff, chewing-gum, fluffy chewing-gum, a dead mouse, money, scissors, books, newspapers – hundreds of objects which were dead to my eyes and hands because not one of them was, conclusively, part of an assassin's equipment. The soprano was proved to be pregnant. Third time through the psalm I found it, a vest-pocket automatic. Its owner, a skinny, sparse-haired tenor, stared at me.

'You can explain this?' I asked.

Then bullets began to shower down from three sides of the courtyard. Automatic rifles.

'Everyone down,' I shouted.

Everyone fell on their faces except the skinny man, who leapt at me and tried to bite through my gun hand. I lifted my arm with him on the end of it, swung him upwards into the air and slammed him down on the cobbles. When I looked up I could see three of them, two men and a woman, standing on the roofs of the palace. They were the two tenors plus contralto who had wheeled away the petrol bomb woman. My mistake, letting them go.

I shouted again: 'Right, when I say run, everyone run to the nearest door.' I paused. 'Right, RUN!'

The archbishop was no runner. I stayed with him, shooting cover as we went, but they shot too well. He kept shouting to me.

'I should never have believed it. Jones, Derickson, Miss Teresa and Forster, all turning against me. Well, Jones *perhaps* but—'

He was hit, once, twice, three times and staggered against me. I tried to hold him but I only had one hand free and he was heavy. He sagged, robes and all, into the basin of a fountain which reminded me of a fountain I'd seen in an Italian travelogue. I pulled his head above water.

He said: 'But I shall be *soaked*.'

Then they got him square in the forehead. There were

goldfish. I got to the phone, called in the Yellows. The snipers held out for three hours. Then the choristers were allowed out to collect their clothes, first the women, then the men, then the boys. You can understand my dissatisfaction with that assignment. But what else could I have done? What would you have done? I came out of that one shaking. I don't know really how to describe what I felt about the archbishop, I hadn't known him for long. But I had the feeling that he was, well, a good old bloke. Let's leave it at that.

Security was unhappy about me. I wasn't exactly reprimanded for the bumping of the archbishop, but I was punished by being sent to Hereford to guard, not a man, but a frozen-meat magnate's collection of paintings.

In my time I have guarded men, women and property. Property has the advantage that it just sits there. You can weave an intricate carpet of security over every inch of a house of treasures, place your booby-traps, electronic spies and bugs among the works of art so that if so much as a tiny Moore is raised from its pedestal, the house is automatically sealed as tight as a rock. Human targets move constantly, they nurse whims which grow up to become obsessions, they are liable to fling themselves over a security barrier to embrace some two-toothed grandma with a flick-knife in her snood, they are prone, especially in business or in love, to try to outwit even their own BGs. Human beings present an ultimately insoluble security challenge, which is one of my main motives for guarding them. Guarding property tends to flatten the mind. Therefore a man who wants his property guarded is well advised to meet his guards often, so that they identify the property with the man.

Let me explain. Say you are set to watch a gallery of pictures which are, to somebody somewhere, worth three million pounds. At first you look at the pictures as pictures, you try to appreciate them to the best of your ability. After a while, however beautiful or instructive they may be, they are liable to prey on your mind as images, intruding on your dreams and recurring in your daytime considerations. So you will probably begin to dislike them and think of them in terms of money in order to render them bearable. Instead of seeing a highland landscape populated by varnished cows, you will see forty thousand pounds hanging in a sixty-pound frame, instead of the squirm of Elvis Presley in blue jeans vividly rendered, you will begin to see one thousand pounds dangling from the picture rail. This is an unhealthy situation. You are thinking of the pictures simply as objects to be sold or stolen or stolen and sold. This sort of thinking can lead to an inside job on your insides turning you from a guardian into a thief. But if the owner of the paintings makes frequent visits, especially with friends who come to look at the paintings, the situation changes for the better. Monotony is broken, the pictures themselves seem to liven up under the comments of their owner, the flattery of his visitors. Most important of all, you begin to identify the pictures with their owner. They become His Highland Landscape, His Elvis in Blue Jeans and so on. They are not merely objects, they are extensions of the owner.

This is not a fanciful way of looking. This is the real importance of property. The true property owner regards his possessions as extra limbs or faculties. I have known an owner who would rather lose his feet than his furniture. And nearly all of them would rather lose their sense of smell than their houses. Wouldn't you? You may argue with this concept of the importance of property, but turn round and face the facts: since violence to an intruder is acceptable if it is applied in the defence of property – and this has been the attitude of all governments in all eras – property must therefore be at least as important as the human body. I am not speaking as a property owner. Property has never been my need. I am speaking as a cool-minded observer.

I can't claim that I was always cool. During my period in the gallery, a daydream began to unfold in my mind. It went something like this: I was ambling along an endless ancient corridor. There were paintings on the walls, of course, most of them hidden under soft blankets of dust, almost like a powder, but some of them were clean enough to reveal at least the eye and cheek of a portrait face, or a minuscule old general on a rearing horse, a few waves of some unnamed ocean or a neat, black-bordered rectangle of abstract yellow. There were also tapestries along the walls, but these were as worn as if they had been used as barrack-room carpets, they might as well have been abstracts. Occasional long threads of different lengths depended from them, shifting in the draught. Paintings and tapestries, these were neither bad nor good, they simply radiated a sense of age, of being tired, or being nearly dead. Life support consumables looking old. The ceiling was the bad part of the picture or daydream. It was vaulted and had been constructed many years ago of thousands of different-sized stones. In parts this ceiling sagged, in other places, apparently at random, it sucked itself upwards. Some stones had shifted downwards and seemed about to fall. A very hard surface but a very soft surface. A mouth of rotting stone. Powder, very finely grained as you got close to it, drifted towards the floor, powder and occasionally flakes from the medieval substance which had been used to stick the stones together so eccentrically. There were some stones which might fall of their own weight and yet leave all the others suspended. There were other stones whose fall would mean the obvious doom of the entire English corridor. Those stonemasons never heard of the Domino Theory. I composed this ghost image of a gallery, but it grew beyond my control and often superimposed itself upon my view of the actual gallery, with its shining paintings and Rentokilled, reinforced ceiling.

Once that daydream took hold on me, it began to twang my nerves. I posted applications for a transfer on the first of every month, but they never came to anything. I started drinking the hard stuff, no water. The first few hours of booze would release me gradually to a world outside that corridor where there seemed to be no difficulty in moving around. But during the next few hours my brain would begin to tense up, the dent in my head which I received at Sir Arthur's house would begin to ache and I would be more desperately aware of the ghost corridor than ever. Now I could understand the drinking habits of General 'Patch'. To escape drinking, I took to driving. Keep going. I invested my savings in a British Cadillac Pirhana and spent my days off playing the motorways, you know what I mean, occasionally veering off to inspect the countryside. One lunchtime, among the dales of the West Riding, I drank straight whiskies in a rather beautiful pub marred only by a skeletonic landlord who spieled stream-of-consciousness gags, many of which struck me as thoroughly subvert. I made a note of his name. As I drove away round narrow corners, I had to weave through groups of hikers on their way back from climbing. They did not all look like hikers to me. The ones who looked most like hikers I suspected most strongly of not being hikers. My frustration, the new anger I had fuelled with whisky, rose in me like sick. Those men on the moon, the first ones, they never got angry, did they? I stopped for the next two hikers, young men of about student age, pressed the electric unlock and let them into the back of my car. I hardly looked at them, I stared at the road ahead as soon as we began to move, I began to argue with them, not stopping for breath or counter-argument:

'So you're walking and you're climbing up rocks. What are you trying to prove? If you want to bash around from place to place, you could get a car, anyone can get a car, if you can't afford a car you could do some bloody work until you can afford a car. It doesn't make you a man or tough or something just because you tramp and slog along, rain or bloody shine, it doesn't make you any bigger or better, you just get there slower. You think you look superior to the families on the road in their cars, you despise them with their children and their dogs, their little radios and picnic baskets and their wallets with five pounds in reserve in case and the whole family's stock of passes and

IDs and work certificates. And you think your heavy shit-covered boots and your shit-coloured rucksacks and your moronic knitted hats make you look special and heroic, little dwarf heroes, pulling yourselves up slabs of wet cold rock and not even a camera to record the scene when you get there, because you're above owning cameras, aren't you? What's so bloody great about you? What's inside you, that's what I want to know?'

They asked me to stop the car. I stopped it and they got out. The ginger moorland around us was totally empty. I picked up my monkey-wrench, swung out of the car, and before ten seconds were out, one two three four five six seven eight nine ten, count them aloud, I had bashed in both their skulls. I dragged them from the verge and left them behind a group of rocks. I felt neither better nor worse. It was a murder. It was not important. I drove back to Hereford that afternoon.

After a year of low gloom in that gallery during which slow-motion masturbation proved the saving of my sanity (I once took four hours not including the lunch-break), I was plucked back by Security for another assignment. My temper was buzzing like a power-mower and I didn't use a silencer. Before Security could even speak I told him:

'If you're thinking of posting me to Hampton Court Maze – bury it. Or maybe you don't want to push me that far down the pyramid? Maybe you want me to play BG to a Dobermann pinscher?'

Security seemed pained.

'You've been recalled to Hollow Hill.'

I did an imitation of applause.

'Who the hell's going to train me? I've done it all. I've seen it all. I know the BG thing in seven hundred and seven positions. I don't need retraining or rehabilitation or retreading. Bury it.'

I pulled out my BG card and threw it on his desk.

'You'll find me guarding the Piccadilly bog.'

A voice behind me said:

'I hope you'll change your mind, Rossman.'

Commander Gray stood there with that old odd smile. He said:

'I've got no argument with your record at all. The point is, I've been asked by the government to move into politics. I've agreed. For the next few months I'll be finishing old business and planning for the future. Then I shall leave Hollow Hill.'

'Are you offering me a job on the teaching staff, sir?'

'No, Rossman. I shall be needing my own personal BGs. And I'll need you, for one.'

I shook Security's hand and then the commander's. It was coming true. As we drove towards Hollow Hill, the commander said:

'How's that portable desert of yours, Rossman?'

'Which desert, sir?'

'That desert of the future you saw in your head.'

'I remember. Well, it's been a bit full of crater-shadows lately. But now it's all lighting up again. Glaring bright.'

He leaned back and closed his eyes. The commander called us to his flat next day. Ten of us sat around drinking iced coffee. Commander Gray would have ten personal BGs, ten fingers, two fists. Among the ten were Jarmyn, leaning forward with his elbows on his knees, and Finn, tilting his chair backwards and widening his eyes at the woman who moved in the background, her white dress exaggerating her tan.

'I'll just skim over the political state of the nation,' said the commander. 'You all know that this country's skidding fast to the edge of a revolution. Examples?'

All of us knew the form with the commander. A one-word question meant that each pupil answered round the class. We spoke up, clockwise.

'Two Rehabilitation Camp mutinies in one year. At least two.'

'Intellectual defections. Er, and exile colonies arming.'

'Morale low in the Yellows.'

The commander: 'Why?'

'Too many of them being picked off by snipers in the cities.'

The commander: 'Plus divided leadership. Plus the fact that Yellow policies have been designed to produce the minimum deep security with the maximum murderous bad will.'

Finn said: 'The curfew's not working. Makes for much more trouble than it cures. It's fucked up the pubs and you can't do that in England.'

'You can add the regional thing – all the country's money being sucked down into the South-East. The Scots, the Welsh and the Northerners get angrier every year. Something's got to blow.'

I said: 'The Rot seems to be uniting.'

The commander nodded. There were three other suggestions, then Jarmyn said: 'Frustration.'

The commander: 'Yes, but what about?'

'Our own government.'

'But doesn't the government take the views of Labour voters and Conservative voters and mash them together and serve them up to everyone's satisfaction?'

'That's the theory. But this government spends all its energy on trying to keep order and it can't even do that.'

'Why?'

'Cutting the crap – lousy leadership.'

Pause. A long pause ended by Finn's laughter. Then the commander laughed too.

'Exactly,' he said. 'Our Prime Minister has been chosen, bred you might say, for his qualities of self-effacement and weakness of will. He is up to his eyes in consensus and he thinks he's drowning and he wants out.'

The PM certainly had appeared increasingly porridgy in recent broadcasts, but we hadn't known he was about to purge himself. The commander waited, so I said:

'So the All-Party Government has asked you to step in?'

'Correct. I'm to be nominated by the Prime Minister as his replacement at the conference next month. So I'm going to need all ten of you, aren't I?'

There was a bang. All ten of us were out of our chairs before we realized that the commander's woman was opening the first of a dozen champagne bottles. As I stared into my glass, that multi-coloured landscape of stone expanded and grew brighter. The commander announced that I'd be in charge of the other nine BGs, but I hardly heard him, I had sensed that already. I watched the surface of my mind, the finely grained desert, exploding into action. It was like turning the pages of a comic book starring a new super-hero – BODYGUARD. Perhaps I would suggest it to one of the big publishing houses, and my monthly adventures would shine from every bookstall in the land. *Bodyguard Versus The Rot*. I was still grinning to myself about this as I stripped off and slipped into bed. I got out again quickly and pulled back the sheets and blankets. My bed was full of custard.

The All-Party Conference was held at Oval City, a Midlands town built only five years before. It was the cleanest town I'd ever known, its main, great oval of a boulevard lined with towers of varying heights, colour-schemes and shapes, their schedule-washed panes reflecting other panes, the colours clashing and mixing. Weighty transparent doors edged with chrome and black rubber, equipped with nervous systems so that they edged apart whenever a person or an object approached, were standard equipment on all buildings, except for the steel slab doors on high-security offices. After a day spent examining the Oval, my dreams were dominated by automatic doors. You would move closer to a shopfront to examine a jacket, the doors would edge open hopefully, a shopman's face would look at you, you would smile and shrug, he would nod without smiling, bored with such mistakes, and you would, looking down for the position of the magic eyes, move out of their beams to let the doors shift back to shut. There's something eerie about non-confrontation like that. And all down the street, the gleam of doors slid open and closed, black throats, shining teeth seen out of the corner of your eye. And I remember a couple of Yellows playing with a door, one of them paddling his foot in and out of the beam, the gap obediently appearing and disappearing, if a gap, which is an absence of door, can be said to disappear. It was only on my second circumambulation of the Oval that I saw a stuck door. Passers-by stopped to look at it, the trapped shop-people and customers gesticulated and a group of kids poked at the magic eyes with their fingers. An old man said to me:

'Someone ought to keep those children away from the Oval. Come here with their bubble-gum and plaster it over the eyes.'

I hadn't thought of that, but it bothered me as I passed the lines of electric cars drinking from their pavement sockets. It was the old vandalism thing – the instinct that seems to strike whenever you try to help people. Give them a fine new city with everything laid on from bowling to Bartok and back again, and out pops the urge towards mess.

We talked about it for some time in the bar of the Powell Hotel, but nobody could push the solution much further than 'Double the Yellows' and nobody cheered that idea. But I want to put it on record that (*a*) Oval City has the most aesthetically pleasing (Colourmix) pavements I have seen and (*b*) Oval City is the only place in Britain where I have seen a teenage gang lower their trousers and shit, concertedly, on the pavement. The boys in the bar nodded when I made this point. Shit gangs were an Oval City speciality, very often they did not waste their loads on concrete, but made use of filing cabinets, electric typewriters, cash registers and desk drawers. The barman told how a clergyman, half an hour before a christening, had found a gallon of sewage in his font. I remarked that the shit gangs were less vulnerable than most saboteurs – you can't arrest people for being full of shit. The barman then made a subvert remark which I reported later but which I will not repeat.

My pre-conference days in the City passed quickly, liaising with the Yellows, double-briefing my own team, especially Finn who was inclined to catnap, tightening security in and around the shining, circular, soaring conference hall. For all its shit gangs, Oval City was the most waterproof town in Britain. All the phones were bugged whether they were off the hook or not and second phones for the bedroom were remarkably cheap and popular. Of course there were public rumours of mass bugging, but sooner or later most subverts forgot, or just got so fed up that they spilled it all in clear to each other (and us) over the line.

The commander's nomination wasn't scheduled until the third and final day of the conference. But naturally I was there on the first two days, drinking it in – not the speeches but the arrangements. The hall itself, a concrete and plasti-glass re-interpretation of the Albert Hall, was ringed by a thick line of Yellows. The commander selected a group of Hollow Hill men to guard the dome and I was in charge inside the hall, where seats spiralled down towards the powerfully-illuminated platform. There were no dark corners. Not only had every delegate of any importance brought his personal BG, but there were plain-clothesmen in the seats on either side of every aisle. Occasionally a large BG would perch on the back of his seat for a better view and when that happened scores of other BGs' heads would jerk in his direction, recognize him and then resume their habit of slowly panning their eyes over the auditorium. Everything looked good to me. Beautiful. Only the delegates seemed nervous. There was toughness in the language of their speeches, most of them arguing for sterner measures against The Rot, but their voices teetered weakly through the sound system. They sounded more worried about their own life-spans than the future of the Community.

On the third day I stood in the wings with the commander. He wore his dark-red uniform and he smiled his small smile as the Prime Minister took the rostrum. As the PM bowed his head to begin, there was a three-minute ovation, but it sounded more like a mixture of sentimentality and obligation than encouragement. He spoke for an hour. The first third of his speech outlined the problems facing Britain. The second third spoke of the need to combat such problems. The final third began with the statement: 'I have decided to submit my irrevocable resignation to this conference.' Then he waited. There was nothing except silence. He continued: 'This country needs a new man, a younger man, to lead Britain out of the shadows of subversion and into the full sunlight of a society without fear. That man must be one whose strength of will is beyond question. He must be a man with an exceptional knowledge of security. He must be a man who stands above and beyond the sectarian strife and dogmatic rivalry which is an inevitable element in party politics. He must be a man who can be trusted by us all, of whatever party, to act in the interests of the State.

'And for this post, I would like to nominate such a man. He has served his country at home and abroad in peace, war and civil strife. My friends, I give you the next Prime Minister of Great Britain – Commander Daniel Gray!'

The soundtrack of the conference churned into chaos for half a minute, then all the delegates were standing, some of them clapping their hands above their heads, BGs were standing on their seats precariously, waving their fists in the air, even the Yellows on the exits were cheering. When the Foreign Secretary tried to second the motion, he could hardly be heard above the urgent, fast-talking caucuses which had suddenly formed all over the auditorium. Delegates were sprinting up and down steps, pausing to whisper two words to a friend and sprinting on to the next ally. As the Foreign Secretary concluded there was a tidal wave of sound. The commander walked to the rostrum and I moved just behind him, leaned across to adjust a couple of microphones for him and took my seat in the row behind the old Prime Minister. Jarmyn, from the front row facing the platform, nodded to me and I grinned back.

The commander began to speak. 'I am not going to waste your time with compliments to the retiring Prime Minister or with flattery of his government. I am only interested in words when words lead to action—'

There was a buzz of electricity. Two of the plexiglass panels in the dome slid back, like those bloody doors. There was a shower of hand-grenades and smoke bombs. I grabbed for the commander as he staggered, forced him to the floor and crouched over him. He jerked below me but I could see no blood. He whispered: 'My chest.' Then Finn was with us, pulling me away from the commander, heaving him into his arms and out through the platform's back door. I looked round quickly before following him. The sprinkler system still wasn't operating, grenades were still falling and there was blood and fire and screaming. A subvert fell from the dome's height and broke across the back of a seat. We took over the first ambulance we found, together with its doctor. I shoved the driver out of his cab so I could drive. Finn stayed in the back with the commander and the doctor. At the hospital I jumped out and opened the back doors. Finn lowered himself to the roadway and put his hands on my shoulders.

I said: 'He's dead.'

Finn shrugged and nodded. The doctor joined us. I said to him:

'Can't you do anything? Transplant or anything? Anything?'

The doctor said: 'There's nothing.'

Although I was crying, I said:

'Listen, doctor. I'm not going to guard his body, I'm going after those murderers. You guard him. Make sure. If anyone mucks about with the commander's body, I'll break your neck.'

Finn said: 'All right, Len, let's go back and get them.'

Back at the hall we found nothing but horror at first. The dead, in their suits, delegates and BGs, were laid along the pavements a hundred yards from the blaze. The last subvert had been sniped off the dome. We saw Jarmyn, an immobile heap on the steps. A couple of Yellows pulled up in a prowler beside Finn.

The driver said: 'Get in, Finn. We've heard that some of those buggers are out at the East Dump.'

Finn climbed in and I followed. There wasn't time to ask questions. We took the East Road out of Oval City fast, pumping the siren, stopping only for roadblocks. The Yellow at the wheel explained to us that four or five miles out of town, to north, south, east and west, were placed four enormous rubbish dumps which not only absorbed all the trash of Oval City, but also served the Midland cities which sprawled around the new town. The road curved over the crest of a low brown hill. We stopped.

Below us lay a ragged-edged bowl of ground, about three miles wide, four miles long. It contained every colour, that surging, frozen lake of junk. But white dominated, the dirty white of ton after ton of newsprint, paper towels, paper napkins, paper tissues, paper everything. Over the surface of that lake hovered a cloud of low-flying pieces of paper. Here and there irregular shapes of brickwork rose above the surface, the remains of the houses which were demolished when Oval City was built. There were other peaks. Mounds of brown – might have been tea-leaves or rotted grass. Rusted old boilers and cars reared up everywhere. There were deep shadows too, some of them apparently filled with water. It was impossible to estimate the depth of the rubbish.

We walked closer. Details unblurred. A horizontal lamp-post. A dump within a dump which consisted of a pile of broken wheels of all kinds. Far away, on the opposite bank, a queue of heavy trucks steaming in the sun, disgorging and retreating. Old trees gone grey. Obsolete TV sets, some with their faces shattered. Hills of dead food. Plastic objects which would last for ages before being absorbed into the mass. A roll of yellow cotton trapped by barbed wire. A landscape dedicated to decay. Desolation, desolation, desolation.

Something moved. An old coat, dark-blue, bloated, right at my feet. Its sleeve moved and then two muscular rats sped out. I turned to Finn and the Yellows:

'Stay at the edge and cover me. I'll see if there's anyone in there.'

Finn motioned the Yellow who hadn't been driving to escort me. I nodded and beckoned the man. I picked up a long thin bar of iron and began to prod the soft, squashed newsprint at the edge of the trash lake's surface. It was safe enough. Once on the dump it became hard to judge distance and even shapes. The eye was dizzied by such chaos. Keep going. We walked up a strip of aluminium to the top of a multi-coloured ridge. Then we saw proof, in two, three and then four widely separated dips of what had been dead ground to us, that the big dump was inhabited. As soon as we were spotted, there was a curious birdlike whistle, very loud, and the small groups of squatting people became, within a few seconds, invisible, disappearing into holes among the rubbish. Since the landscape was so confused and senseless, it was hard to keep a fix on where they'd disappeared, but by orienting on a patch of water we reached one of the inhabited dips. I kept my hand gripped on my gun as I called them out. There had been three figures, but only one emerged, from a huge iron pipe which jutted out of the depths at an angle of forty-five degrees. He was a young, balding and bearded tramp. His identity card, which he found after much fumbling, smelt rancid, it was folded and ingrained with sweat. The Yellow at my shoulder whispered:

'There's a lot of oddies lurking in the big dump. Some of them are tramps.'

I nodded. 'This is a funny kind of tramp.'

The young tramp swept at his hair, which was dirty yellow, with both hands. His face muscles jerked and he began a little crooning moan. I faced him.

'How many people live in this dump?'

He stared at me, continuing to moan, and then his moaning stuttered and became something between speech and crying.

'Pl – place – mur here – ther place wern – gizz . . .' he burbled on while I waited for his words to begin to make sense. When I'd waited long enough and still no information, I said:

'I don't think you're a moron and we're going to take you in. You're going where you'll learn to talk better sense.'

The Yellow stepped forward, walking between me and the tramp, bringing forward his handcuffs. A bad mistake. The tramp whipped out a short, heavy iron bar and cracked the Yellow's forehead wide open. He was quick and he was certainly not a moron. As my bullets brought him down he was shouting, using real words, to his friends. As I bent towards him to make sure, a bullet passed over my shoulder. I turned in time to see a face disappear in a cliff of newspaper. Then a shot from the right-hand side nicked my wrist. It seemed to have come from a railway carriage lying on its side. I turned in time to see the face in the cliff again, took a shot but the face pulled back into its tunnel. A light-brown face with a black beard. I was crouching, scared. Because I was still in the dip where the tramp's friends had been. Any moment they might shoot from any of the thousand shadows in this basin of rags and crap. I couldn't see Finn or the Yellow driver anywhere. I had to assume they'd been picked off by snipers. So the nearest point of safety now seemed to be the far edge of the dump, where the huge lorries tipped their cargoes. I began to run. The shots behind me became more frequent. It was bad running. Too many loops of wire. Sometimes my foot would sink into mashed cloth or slime. And suddenly it became the charge of the light brigade because they were shooting from all sides. Two seconds later I crashed through the roof of an unoccupied tunnel. The shots stopped, whistling began, a conversation in bird noises.

Now I was below the shifting, slowly mounting waves of the dump, crawling along a tube of a tunnel walled with stink, a hundred damp bad smells. The tube became a roofed trench, almost high enough for me to walk in without lowering my head, its banks shored up with broken branches of furniture, occasional holes above admitting pillars of sun, small clouds of steam rising from the overheated floor. Eggshells crackled under my shoes. A bedspring jagged a hole in my jacket. First World War, I said to myself, but there was no mud and, for the moment, no gunfire. My tunnel swerved and divided into three apertures. It would matter which I chose, but I had no way of choosing. I had to keep going, keep going if I was ever going to reach the other side of the dump. More crawling, then a wade through brown slime, First World War, and once, just behind me, an avalanche of old shoes. The tunnel grew deeper and darker, the props more frequent and stronger, beams of wood now, and the ventilation came down drainpipes rather than random holes. I turned a corner and found myself in a subterranean hall.

I surrendered. It was no use trying to shoot it out. There were too damn many of them and all of them, men and women in their rags, armed with businesslike guns. I laughed, not at the people, but at the ludicrously huge cavern they'd created. Its main supports, two massive oblongs of metal, had once been double-decker buses. Girders, ladders and planks connected the roofs of the buses and had been covered with netting, wire and mattresses, which were covered in their turn with multiform rubbish. These rag people had hollowed out a valley in the heart of the dump, dragged two discarded buses into the hollow, levered them upright and then constructed around them not only this soggy cave, but also a system of communications which probably spread throughout the dump. Under my laughter I was furious at the cancer in Oval City's security. Everyone knew that huge dumps like this existed in the wasted parts of Britain, and everyone knows that dumps attract scavengers. So had security said to itself: Leave the tramps alone, they're in the dumps where they should be, rot to rot and no harm done?

Harm is always done by neglect, there is no neutral area, there can be no no-man's-land in the whole universe. Subverts are desperate, especially in a fully-bugged New City, and their desperation must be taken into account everywhere, or they'll even grow gills and spawn in the ocean. They took my gun and turned it against me, pushing me in front of them into the lower deck of the nearest bus. My pockets were searched and my papers taken upstairs by a boy of about twelve. Two men kept out of reach, gun-barrels aimed at my head. A ginger-haired girl came downstairs and motioned me to sit. She took the seat behind me. A stubbled black took the seat in front. Nobody said anything at first, as Ginger scanned my papers and then passed them over to Black. When he'd finished, he said:

'So you've been a Yellow and now you're a BG?'
Ginger: 'Who's your target?'
'I don't know who you are.'
Black: 'You don't need to know anything about us. What are you here for?'
'I came to try to find some people.'
Ginger: 'What people?'
'You may be the people I want to see.'

Then I saw Annie Beauvais in the doorway. So I jumped, hands outstretched, for Black's neck. The bullets hit me in midair. After that, whatever happened, I was brought to this room. I don't remember who rescued me or how I got here or anything like that, I was unconscious with the pain and the wounds and the shock. Later, I suppose, I was unconscious with drugs.

I like this room. I don't mind the bandage round my eyes. The bed-pan's awkward. I want to be helpful. Today my body feels very calm. My mind, too, is calm, but it cannot think difficult things. It moves slowly as if it was afraid of falling over. Some days I know that I'm very agitated and my mind moves too fast. Some days I cannot remember however hard I try, I do not know what I have said or done. I have a feeling that I am being used. I want to be useful.

How do you feel generally?
Warm.
Where does the warmth come from?
My stomach, it seems to be my stomach. But there are sometimes shadows. The shadows are very cold.
You're not in any pain?
Sometimes. Not now. Sometimes when the last injection's wearing off. Sometimes I'm in pain in my dreams. I think I was shot with my own gun. How many things, you know, bullets?
Three bullets.
That's a lot, three. You know they walked on the moon. I didn't. I was sitting watching their arms go all long. Bits of moon sticking up out of the ground. They put up a flag. It was a funny flag because of there being no air. They did little jumps. It was awful, I wasn't there.
You were a boy in those days.
I didn't move my eyes away from the screen. While they were on the moon I pissed in a tin so I could watch them all the time they were on the moon. Oh it tore me in two, being down here.
He said: 'It's hard to tell whether it's a cloud or a rock.'
They were on the surface.
That's good.
Is it daytime or night-time?
Night.

Afterword

LEN ROSSMAN died of his wounds several days after dictating the end of his narrative. During the time I sat by his bedside encouraging him to talk, the strangest thing about him was his lack of curiosity. He never asked about events in the world outside. He never even recognized my voice. This was just as well.

He would not have spoken at all if he'd known that 'The Rot' which he hated had broken into open revolution throughout Europe, that the Revolution was destined to continue, to grow and to triumph, that Commander Gray, unharmed during the storming of the conference, was one of the Revolution's most active instigators and that I was one of its thousands of agents.

Rossman's narrative is both single-minded and rambling, a tangle of facts and fantasies, distorted sexuality, obscured dates, anti-feminism, glorified brutality and narcissism. We publish it now, in the fifth year of the European Revolution, because it reflects some of the insanity of pre-revolutionary England.

I have edited Rossman's narrative extensively. His tape-recordings are full of repetitions, hesitations and incomprehensible passages. These I have excised. But I have cut not one word for political reasons. I have even included my own (italicized) exchanges with Rossman in hospital, whenever these seem marginally relevant to the understanding of this man and his kind.

FINN MURDOCH